A Near Miss

Jami Lynn Viviers

◆ FriesenPress

Suite 300 - 990 Fort St
Victoria, BC, V8V 3K2
Canada

www.friesenpress.com

ISBN
978-1-03-910697-0 (Hardcover)
978-1-03-910696-3 (Paperback)
978-1-03-910698-7 (eBook)

1. BISAC *Fiction, Romance, Contemporary*

Distributed to the trade by The Ingram Book Company

Chapter 1

S eraphina St. Clair; the woman who has it all; well, that is what everyone thinks anyway. She founded her own consulting firm and made it and her one of the most sought-after strategic consulting firms. She was also a bit of an artist who preferred to focus on contemporary art with bold lines and the mixing of colors. Every time she painted there was something that spoke to her creating the paintings she did. And she loved car racing. Going to local tracks watching some of the young up-and-comers race their hearts out for the win, and a chance to be scouted out was one of her favorite activities as she followed the racing circuit. Yes, she had a very full and productive life.

However, due to her workaholic habits, taking her work everywhere she went, including home, she hadn't the time to find that someone to love, grow old and have children with. She was about to enter her forties and figured her time was up and had resigned herself to nights spent alone, working on whatever project she had on the go. She shook her head to clear her thoughts, as she took her glass of wine and took a sip. Raising her glass, "Darling, these are the last few days before you enter that damn decade of 40; make them count!" she said to herself with more conviction than she felt before taking another sip of her wine.

She was not overly tall with long dark hair, almost black except for one lock of hair over her right temple; that was white. She always had that one piece for as far back as she could remember. She had asked her doctor about it some years ago and he said sometimes hair would lack the pigment cells to color hair. She had the most beautiful dark eyes; a deep espresso and were almond shaped. Her complexion, a beautiful and unique shade that most women were jealous of and lips that always seemed to have a smile waiting just under the surface. She was a beauty of unknown exotic origin. There were some individuals who asked if she was a model because of her beauty. Seraphina refused to use her looks to get ahead in life, preferring honest hard work, and a whole lot of determination.

Her early years were not all that great, and she had worked very hard to leave it all behind her, not looking back at everything she endured as a child. She refused to let those old demons control her, and why she worked so hard to this day; it was what she used as her therapy. Work. Working hard to help companies restructure, be viable and ensure share-holders wouldn't bail when times became difficult. All companies had to be seen actively doing something to cut costs, delete duplications, and evaluate every process.

She did have one guilty pleasure that she greatly enjoyed: stock car racing. She loved the smell of rubber, racing gas, the roar of the engines, and feeling the rumble as the cars raced past the fans watching in the stands. Her goal was to attend two races per season; sometimes that was difficult. She loved to watch the fans gather around their favorite drivers wanting selfies, autographs, and that once in a lifetime opportunity to talk with them. She did not have a favorite driver or race team, just a love for the sport as a whole. It was something she had stumbled on by pure chance on TV one Sunday afternoon years and years ago. Since then, she loved to watch them speed around the different tracks trying to figure out the strategy of the teams and guessing when a caution would happen.

On this Thursday evening however, she was wrapping up a project that she had to endure. Actually, it felt more like torture for her. Working on this project had left her feeling drained and anxious. The CEO was a bully who thought women did not belong in board rooms. She knew she was smarter than he was, and he took every opportunity to try and humiliate her. Her final gift to this company would include firing this CEO and finding one who better matched their vision. The board wanted new and fresh, and as long as that idiot was still there, that would never happen. Once she finished her final report, she placed it aside looking at the three binders, all marked accordingly with her very long list of changes that needed to be made or the company could be bankrupt within six months. 'God, I hope my next project won't be like this; I'm getting tired of fighting the old boys' clubs; they have to realize that their attitudes are their own demise.'

Chapter 2

*I*t was unusually cold for the middle of November as Seraphina drove towards a potential clients' location in North Carolina. While she loved to travel and experience the different local cultures, it was the weather that would always get to her. "Ugh, heavy sleet," she muttered as she drove, paying careful attention to the roads while being passed by someone going much too fast for the conditions. 'Jesus, there's an accident ready to happen; the further south I go the crazier they seem to be,' she thought while shaking her head as another car passed her making her look at her own speedometer. "Well, I'm not the slow-poke at least," she said seeing that her own speed was also above the posted limit.

She eventually made it to a very large campus-like facility with a guard waiting at the gate. She pulled up to the guard, rolled down her window and handed him her driver's license and business card. "Good morning, Mr. Brandon is expecting me," she told him with a smile.

The guard returned her license with a parking pass and visitor badge while explaining to her where the main parking lot was located.

Seraphina pulled into the numbered parking spot she was assigned and turned off the rental. "Well," she said, looking at the building before her, "this should prove to be very interesting indeed."

She collected her briefcase, making sure it had everything she would need before getting out of the car and walking towards the entrance. She had a feeling of excitement and a little apprehension; this was an iconic campus in a top tier of the stock car racing scene, and she wondered what she could offer this huge company.

Once inside, she was met by a lady, who introduced herself as Sally who would escort her to Mr. Brandon's office. Seraphina noted that the person guiding her had shortened her boss's name and wore business casual attire. She put that into her mental note's column under culture.

"Good morning, I'm Seraphina St. Clair," she said to Mr. Brandon as he extended his hand while Sally left closing the door behind her.

Mr. Joseph Brandon and Seraphina got to work discussing the company and what he would like her to do for his company. He wanted to restructure and make the various processes easier and streamlined. He also wanted a solid succession plan. That surprised Seraphina to hear of a succession plan; that was one area most clients did not want her to touch. While they talked, her brain was in overdrive with the different pieces that were being presented to her. She was taking notes, thankfully knowing shorthand to help her keep up with the conversation and her brain.

Mr. Brandon adjourned the meeting, saying he needed a break. She understood as they had been working for three hours now. "How about I have Jason show you around the campus and explain how we currently run the shops and maybe you can see what changes can happen quickly and without disruption," he said.

"That sounds great, I would love to see how your business currently runs," she replied, getting up and noting she was quite stiff from sitting still too long. She walked out of Mr. Brandon's office to see Sally waiting for her just outside the door; she wondered how she knew of the break in the meeting. She also tucked that away to figure out later. Sally mentioned that Jason would only be a bit longer as he was wrapping up a phone conversation. This gave Seraphina an opportunity to have a look about the lobby, seeing photos of the various wins the company had through the years. Some of the photos brought back memories of being at the track; the smell of rubber and gas, hearing the engines brought a smile upon her face.

"Hello Seraphina, I'm Jason Knecht." She heard a man say. She turned to see Jason walking towards her.

"Hello, very good to meet you," she responded, shaking his hand. "You're supposed to give me the grand tour, correct?"

"That I am, what would you like to see first?" he offered, ushering her out of the office.

The tour was formal in nature with Jason explaining the layout and how things were done. However, his explanations were superficial in nature. She knew the basics and wanted to get down to the complicated things in the business. Seraphina found Jason to be quite reserved as she knew he would be. He was a champion crew chief for one of the best racing teams in the series. She knew he was very smart, and he knew more than he was letting on to her. What she wanted though, was to break through to find the person behind the façade he showed the public; she had a hunch there was more than the normal press sheet information.

That evening, Seraphina was in her hotel suite working on all the information she had collected, putting it into order for her to study. Her day at the facility was well spent as she had met several individuals, some she knew from watching some of the races, and talked with a few people that she thought could bring her an angle that was away from the corporate package she was given. Jason had shown her the entire facility; the different buildings and explained why they were separated the way they were.

Her gut though, was telling her that there was more information than she was given. Normally, she took her gut instincts into consideration, like her head and heart. Shaking her head from her straying thoughts, she realized her gut, head and heart were all saying the same things; Brandon Motorsports is hiding something. She hoped that whatever it was would be resolved once the final contract had been signed, "Could be they don't want to scare you off, right? Or they could be in worse shape than they have let on," she replied to the thoughts in her head.

She had many thoughts going through her mind about the company, and what processes could potentially be changed. One thought that was tripping her up was the succession plan; why did this company not have one? Every time one of her thoughts trailed through her mind map, it got stuck between the top and the middle layers of management.

"Geez, this is going to suck the life right out of me," she muttered to herself looking at the time. "And now that it's almost pumpkin time Cinderella, you better put this away until later. Its time now to shift gears for tomorrow."

Chapter 3

$\mathcal{T}$he morning of day two in North Carolina was bright and sunny, although still chilly with the wind. "At least all the crap from yesterday is gone from the roads," she said as she drove in the opposite direction from yesterday. As she drove, she wondered about the potential client she was about to meet; they were in the same industry as yesterday's client. In fact, they were competitors in the same series. She wondered what they were looking for and was especially wondering about a certain man that had provided her with many fantasies over the years. 'This should prove to be very interesting indeed.' she thought as she drove up to the guard at the gate.

As she got out of the car, a man came out of the building and walked towards her, "Hi, I'm Ryder, owner of this place, and you must be Seraphina." he said with a smile and reached his hand out to shake hers and take her briefcase.

"Well, hello, yes, I am." Seraphina was slightly surprised to see the man with dark hair and eyes, and his signature 'bad boy' vibe known as Ryder Durand; one of several who competed in the premier series. 'I just might be in serious trouble,' she thought to herself seeing the man in person and up close. Seraphina was also pleasantly surprised that he was waiting to meet her at the door. She put that into her mental notes for later. While they walked towards his office, there was a large assortment of memorabilia on the walls, and not all of it was related to the company either; some of the memorabilia was racing in general. Ryder ushered her into his office and pulled out a chair at a table near the window. Once she was settled, he sat across from her at the table and pulled out a large accordion file that was full of papers. "Oh wow, what do you have for me in there?" she asked, looking at the huge file.

"This is the company: our current business plan, succession plan, and so much more. I am very happy that you agreed to meet with me to discuss how you can help us be more competitive on the business side so we can continue for years to come," Ryder said. "I did a lot of research and found your company; you have an amazing track record and why I contacted you to help us."

"I wondered how you decided on a small company from Seattle to consult for you. All this information we will need, however, before I begin to wade through all of this material, I would like to talk to you about the company, what you see as the issues and your plans for the direction you would like this company to take," she replied, pulling out her notebook to begin recording their conversation.

The two worked through the morning talking about what Ryder wanted to see for the company compared to how it's currently running. Seraphina was so absorbed in everything that Ryder was talking with her about that she was surprised when she heard her phone chime indicating lunch and the need to eat. "Oh wow, look at the time," she said, pulling her phone from her briefcase. "I didn't realize it was lunch already."

"How about we grab some lunch at a nearby restaurant, and this afternoon I will give you the tour of our facility." Ryder offered, getting up from where he was sitting.

Ryder gave Seraphina a very in-depth tour of the facility. She noted that most resources were already pooled together there were and not a lot of duplications. The big exceptions were the race teams themselves which she expected. Ryder explained the reasoning behind the layout and how his company did things; he was very open in his conversation with her and did not leave much out when talking about the company.

Later that evening, Seraphina was in her suite going over the enormous amount of information she was given that day. She had to admit to herself that Ryder was quite the charmer. She knew of him prior to meeting him, however, tried hard to reserve any kind of judgment until she had met him even though he sometimes featured in her dreams.

While sifting through some documents, her mind wandered to Ryder; his school-boy smile, his eyes dancing with amusement and hearty laugh. "Yup, this one is not going to be easy either," she said, shaking herself from her thoughts with a smile dancing across her lips.

Chapter 4

On this third day in North Carolina, Seraphina had two potential clients that she now had to work on and decided to allocate six hours per client. From there, she could develop a plan of action and needs in terms of personnel and technology to be the most effective and efficient at her job. She worked from her suite, preferring the low noise of the radio tuned to some station she was not paying attention to. This was how she worked; noise in the background, at a large table loaded with documents in an order that she knew, writing notes in her iPad as she went through each pile.

She started on her first client, Brandon Motorsports. Mr. B, as she was told to call him, wanted a solid succession plan and to streamline the company. There were many duplications as he had divided the company into two; one 'shop' each per two race teams. The only things that were shared were the corporate offices regarding Human Resources, Finance, IT, and Legal; everything else was duplicated. She wondered if deleting the duplications would help or hinder the company. Streamlining meant doing away with such duplication. She thought about the current culture at Brandon Motorsports, and if they would accept such a major change. "Egads, this is going to be a mess," she said as she stretched her back. "Dammit, I stooped too long," she rasped out as she went to her purse to find her medication for her back spasms.

While she waited for her medication to kick in, she was trying to do the exercises she was told to do when her back decided to hate her and exercise its existence. "This is when I could use a man to deep massage my back and make my muscles behave," she muttered softly as she walked about her suite. "I bet I could find a therapeutic massage clinic nearby that does acupuncture," she thought out loud as she picked up her phone and looked up nearby places. Once she had gotten an appointment, she looked at the time, and decided that it was time to shift her focus to her other client for a bit. She needed to get a handle on them before her conference call to her team back home in Seattle. She had to know exactly what she would need for each team before she put in her order to her counterpart.

"This is going to be so much harder than it looks on paper," she mused as she turned to the other table loaded with Durand Brand Racing's documents. She looked at the papers for a minute, trying to decide where the best place would be for her to tackle first. 'Maybe start at the top and go from there,' she thought for a bit before taking her iPad and moving to a new file for her to begin her notes.

Ryder wanted that elusive competitive edge for the company, and especially his racing teams. She methodically went through the material she was provided and noted that the documents were in great shape as was their current budget. "A strategic edge in an industry that is so heavily regulated is the unicorn among the horses," she spoke out loud. "And I don't have a clue where to even start looking for that unicorn."

It was nearly time for her appointment as her phone reminded her with its chime. "Already?" she said to herself straightening her back and feeling even more spasms course down through her hips with a severe tightening of her muscles. "Dammit; when will I bloody well learn not to do that!" she groaned as she tried to walk about her suite, breathing deeply as she was told to help ease some of the pain. "Oh, god it hurts," she whispered, picking up the phone in her suite to order a car service to take her to the appointment. 'No way can I drive myself there, I feel like I'm eighty. Oops, going to need my cane too,' she thought looking for where she had put the damn thing.

While she waited for her name to be called, she looked about the clinic she had found. It looked like someone's personal space with plants, soothing music, an assortment of chairs to choose from depending on what hurt, and she could hear a water fountain as well. She tried hard not to think about her back; and had her eyes closed, focusing on her breathing when she heard someone call her name. Thinking it was the therapist calling her name, she scrunched her face trying to gather the courage to move when she opened her eyes to see Jason sitting before her with a concerned look on his face.

"Oh! Hi; I thought you were the therapist," she said, catching her own surprise.

"It's fine; you look like you're in a lot of pain," Jason said, taking in her pain-streaked face, and noting the cane held tightly in her right hand.

"Yea, I have back and hip issues, and I spent way, way too long stooped over a couple of tables filled with documents," she said. "Work never ends, and my clients demand quick results."

"I get that; but I think this might be more than expected," Jason said, showing concern on his face.

Seraphina snickered at that comment and before she could reply, heard her name being called from the therapist this time. She moved her cane to help herself up when she felt strong arms gently help her to a standing position. "Thank you so much for your help," she said as she slowly followed the therapist to the room.

Two hours later, Seraphina slowly walked from the therapy room to pay for her treatment of a massage and acupuncture. While she waited a moment for the person ahead to complete his transaction, she felt someone come up behind her. She turned to see Jason standing there. "Are you stalking me?" she asked with amusement.

Jason snickered as he said, "No; I come here twice a week to ensure I don't wind up like you are today."

"Ah, good man; it's much too late for me; but if I can get the pain to subside, then I think, I'm golden," she replied as she moved up to complete her transaction.

Once she was finished, she moved to the side to let Jason move up to the counter, "Have a good evening Jason," she said as she moved to walk out the door.

While she was in the lobby, she was on hold with the hotel trying to get a car service to come and get her so she could return to her suite and soak in a hot bath. "Ugh, I hate waiting," she murmured as she listened to the music in her ear and tapping her foot.

"I can take you back to your hotel." She heard from behind her.

She turned and saw Jason standing behind her with a cute grin on his face. "Oh no, that's fine, thank you. I'm on hold for my car service," she replied.

"It's no problem, really, I can take you back to your hotel," Jason insisted.

Seraphina thought for a moment, determining how long the car service would take. "Thank you; I really appreciate it," she said, accepting his offer and hanging up the phone.

She turned to walk out of the lobby with him, and she felt his hand on her back, gently guiding her to his vehicle. There, he opened the passenger door for her, and while holding the door, helped her into his SUV.

The drive to the hotel was quiet except for the low music from the radio. "How long have you been doing consulting work?" Jason asked, while they were stopped at a red light.

"Hmm, let's see; I started this company over five years ago. I was looking for a career change and thought about it before jumping in and creating my own company," she replied.

"That's interesting; what did you do before then?" he asked.

Seraphina sighed, "I used to work for the government," she told him trying to be evasive.

"Oh? Doing what?" Jason asked, sounding interested.

"Uh, I guess you could say international relations," she replied, hoping that would be the end of this. "What about you? Have you always worked for racing teams?"

"Yea, pretty much; my dad had a team and I helped him out on the weekends, and when I finished school, I was picked up by Brandon Motorsports. I've been here ever since," he replied as he pulled into the hotel's drop off zone.

He parked and turned off the car before getting out and going around helping Seraphina out of his vehicle. She accepted his offered hand as she slowly moved from her seat.

"Thank you so much for the ride back; I appreciate it and your time," she spoke with a warm smile.

"Of course, it's not a problem," he replied as he escorted her towards the door of the building, again with his hand resting gently on the small of her back, feeling her tight muscles move as she walked.

"Have a good evening Jason and thank you again," she replied as she pushed the button for her floor.

"You as well, Seraphina," he responded as he watched her walk onto the elevator, noting the floor, and watching the doors close. "I think I'm in trouble," he mumbled to himself, still staring at the elevator doors.

Chapter 5

This morning Seraphina had a meeting with her staff. She spent the better part of yesterday working on her needs list for the two new clients. While both had some similar desires in terms of streamlining and reducing costs, they also had differences that they wanted to have looked at very carefully. Now, it was her turn to determine what would be needed for each client; what could be shared, and what areas would need dedicated staff. She also had to submit her final quote to each client prior to beginning the actual work, and this was where things got sticky. If you wanted top notch results, you had to pay for them, and she was not cheap. The cost for her to meet and determine needs was the first quote which was usually around the ten-thousand-dollar mark. To do the actual job, depending on the needs and desires of the client could run into the millions.

Her meeting with her staff determined what she thought was going to happen. This morning, both new clients added a time restriction that would double, and for one almost triple the quote, causing Seraphina to rethink her requirements for the quote to the two clients. "Fishizzle, this is not going to be fun," she said to her counterpart, right-hand and best friend, Grant.

"Yea, I see that; and it can't be helped. They decided on a stupid timeline and told us this morning; it is not our fault that the resources needed are going to skyrocket the cost for them. If they want this, then they must pay. They can pay, right?" Grant asked her.

Seraphina laughed, "Yes, they can pay, however, it will put one client past their planned budget for the coming year, so I'm not sure if they will agree," she said.

"Well, what if you were to present them with two quotes; one with their timeline, and one that fits into their budget but, it will be on our timeline," Grant said.

"I was thinking that from the beginning; the one client wants a solid succession plan; that's going to be very difficult as we will likely have to look at resources outside the org," she said, making notes.

"I saw that; they really don't have a succession plan?" he asked.

"Nope; they do not, and for them to continue like this is careless. So, either way, we have our work cut out for us for the next three months at the very least," she said, closing her eyes, imagining all the work that would be required from her and her company.

"You can say no," Grant reminded her, knowing how she worked and thought.

"True, I can; but this is quite a challenge, and it could open up other avenues for us to expand upon," she replied.

"I'm thinking you should focus on one client at a time; granted they are in the same industry, but what they want is very different, and the timeline they both want I think is undoable," he said. "It's going to cause severe burn-out for you and some other key consultants."

"Ugh, I know and I'm already struggling here," she muttered, with pain.

"What happened?" he asked, concerned.

"My back and hips of course; yesterday was hell and I found a place for treatment. Today is a whole new day filled with pain I seriously do not want to deal with," she replied, feeling her body keenly this morning.

"Well, maybe this is telling you it's time to back off for a bit," he said gently. "You've been working way too hard, and too long; I think you should be taking it easy."

"Grant, please leave that alone?" she asked. "I am not going to take time off because my body decided it hates me. You know I have been dealing with this for years and years; its fine! Nothing drugs and treatment can't do to take the edge off" she huffed.

"I know you've been dealing with this for years; I was with you the last time you got hurt. But there does come a time when you do have to slow down. You know this, and Kelley has been worried about you and your worsening pain," Grant reaffirmed.

"Jesus, now I remember why I don't have a husband; you fit the bill nicely and without the sex part," she grumbled, rubbing her face.

Grant laughed, "Hey, you saying I have two wives? I'll be sure to tell Kelley that, and I'll have to figure out how to divide my full attention between you and her!" he teased.

"She knows; and you already divide your attention between the both of us. I told her you nag me worse than she nags at you," Seraphina snickered. "She thinks it's funny how you're worse to me than she is to you."

"So, wife number two, what are you going to do then?" Grant asked with a snicker.

Seraphina rolled her eyes and sighed loudly with a smile on her lips, causing Grant to laugh, "Lets draft up two quotes for each client and let them decide; be sure to add the thirty percent surcharge for the expedited timeline and fifty percent for doubling of required resources."

"Already on it; you will have them first thing in the morning," Grant said before he hung up.

"Ok then, in the meantime, I need to figure out how to work with all this hellish pain today," she whispered as she leaned back in her chair, thinking of what may lay ahead.

Chapter 6

The afternoon of day five, Seraphina had meetings scheduled with each client to present them with the quotes for her company to complete the work asked of her firm. Both quotes were very high in terms of cost, and she knew that the meetings this afternoon were not going to be much fun. Then, add in her body misbehaving was going to make this to be pure torture for her.

She decided on taking a car service to each client instead of trying to drive herself. Grant was efficient as usual; two complete sets of quotes for each client. The first one, being exactly what they wanted, and in the time frame they mentioned; the second one was what they wanted, but with a reasonable timeline and resources with a considerable decrease in costs to the respective company. She was not too sure which would be decided upon or even if the clients would even accept the quotes and find another consulting firm to do the job at a fraction of the cost. She knew there were a few out there who would try to do the same job as her. However, on more than one occasion, she had been hired to clean up their mess.

'God help me on this; these jobs could really make the company, and please help me deal with this pain, it's going to be the death of me,' she sent the thought up as she finished placing the needed items in her briefcase and finding her cane. She managed to make her way down to the lobby of her hotel to find her car service waiting for her.

"First is Brandon Motorsports please," she told the driver as she settled into the comfortable back seat of the luxury vehicle.

She watched the scenery pass by taking in the green of the grass and trees. When she arrived, took a deep breath preparing herself to move from the seat to a standing position. The door opened and she moved to get out when she felt strong arms gently helping her. She looked up to see Jason there with a smile.

"Well, hello," she said, surprised he was there. "Thank you again for helping me."

"Oh, think nothing of it; I was just coming back from a meeting and saw you in the back of the car," he replied as he escorted her into the building, carrying her briefcase.

"You have to be stalking me," she responded with mirth in her voice.

"I promise you, I am not," he said, smiling, "What brings you here today?"

"Today is the day I provide the quote to the company for what they want me to do, with the time and resources that will be required to do the job properly and efficiently while being very concise and diligent. I'm pretty much going to see if I will be working or not," she told him.

"Ah; you're seeing Mr. B this afternoon," Jason said as he led her to the executive offices.

"Yes, I am, and then I have another meeting on the other side of town later this afternoon," she said, again feeling his hand on the small of her back.

It made her feel warm and secure; and she wanted to lean into the person whose hand was on her back. It was something she was not used to feeling, and something she needed to think more about as it was confusing her too.

"Here you are Seraphina, good luck with the meeting," Jason said when they reached the office.

"Thank you, Jason," she replied as she turned to walk into Mr. Brandon's office.

She emerged from the office several hours later feeling exhausted. Her pain level was still high even though she had taken her medication prior to the meeting. She was also feeling frustrated, 'Why, oh why can't these companies realize it costs money to get their shit in order,' she thought as she walked towards the entrance.

Seraphina was so absorbed in her own thoughts that as she walked to the car, nearly missed seeing Jason running towards her, calling out her name, "Hey, hope the meeting was good. I have a question I would like to ask you," he said in a rush crouching down to be eye level with her.

"Sure, what do you want to ask?" she responded, settling herself into the back seat.

"What are you doing for dinner tomorrow evening?" he asked.

Seraphina was slightly surprised by the request and took a moment to focus on his request. "I'm sorry, but I cannot date clients, it creates a conflict of interest," she said, using her usual go-to. It wasn't that she was not interested, but Jason's timing was not all that great.

She had gotten the green light from Mr. Brandon for the expedited quote, and now, she had to push everything into high gear for this specific client.

"What about as friends?" Jason asked, hoping she would agree. "You have to eat," he gently pushed.

Seraphina snickered at that, "Fine; I might manage dinner, but it will have to be later in the week, is that alright?" she replied, taking in his hazel eyes with gold flecks.

"Of course, that will be fine, let me know which evening," Jason confirmed, feeling his heart leap for joy as he closed the car door.

Seraphina told the driver the next stop, and then snickered while slightly, shaking her head. "Ah, if anything, this could be fun," she murmured as she settled in to watch the scenery pass her by once again.

Chapter 7

$\mathcal{R}$yder was impatiently waiting for Seraphina to arrive. He was taken with her exotic beauty and how she carried herself the very first time he saw her. He had tried for the last day or so to come up with some sort of reason to meet up with her and failed to find one. Ryder silently shook his head, knowing that he was way out of her league. She was super smart, had her own company, and had this way with other people; commanding, yet confident, and he learned she had a dry sense of humor where sarcasm was the preferred medium. When he saw the car pull up to the door, he felt his heart leap into his throat, "Here goes nothing," he said to himself as he walked out to greet her.

She felt the car come to a stop, and realized she had dozed off, "Oops," she murmured as she looked to see she was at Durand Brand Racing. "Game face kiddo," she whispered to herself, seeing Ryder come out to greet her.

The car door opened, and Ryder was there to help her out of the car, "Hi there," she said as he took her briefcase from her and guided her to his office.

"How have you been? Are you alright? I see you're using a cane today. Is there anything I can help you with?" Ryder said in a rush.

"I'm fine, thank you. Just back and hip issues that decided to make my life so much fun," she said with a small laugh, trying to write off her need for a cane.

"Are you sure? You look like you're in pain," Ryder said, showing true concern in his voice.

"I've had these issues for years now; I am fine, trust me," she replied, trying to alleviate his concern.

"Somehow, I don't believe that you're fine," he muttered, more to himself.

Seraphina laughed, "Ryder, I am in pain, and have been for years. I have learned to deal with it, and sometimes, that means working through the pain. I'm sure you understand that," she said looking at him with a raised eyebrow as he gently helped her to sit.

Ryder caught the look, and knew what she was talking about, "You know about that huh? Yea, it hurt like hell, but the pain eventually went away as it healed, and I was able to get physiotherapy done," he told her, still looking concerned.

"Exactly, you know what it's like, and just like you, I will get through this," Seraphina replied as she pulled out two large folders as Ryder sat across from her, "Shall we get started?" she asked, going into business mode.

This meeting was particularly long, as Ryder insisted on going through both proposals asking questions and making alternative suggestions. Seraphina hadn't realized how late it had gotten when there was a knock on the office door interrupting their work.

He got up to answer the door to find his secretary with dinner. "Perfect, thank you Francine," Ryder said, accepting the cart with their dinner.

"Oh, my goodness, is it really that late already?" Seraphina said, looking at the cart then her phone, seeing that it was indeed quite late.

"Yes, it is, I know how I work and knew this meeting would take longer than you had probably allocated," Ryder said as he lifted the covers to their dinner. "It isn't high gourmet, but this is seriously good, and one of my favorites."

"What do we have," she asked, curiously smelling something good.

"It's Indian," he replied as he brought over her plate with utensils and napkins, "I hope you like Indian."

"I do; I love the spice, and it's one of my favorites," she replied, feeling her tummy demand the food that was in front of her.

"Excellent," Ryder said as he sat down with his own plate of food.

He kept the conversation light and easy, not wanting to dive too fast or deeply into her world, wanting to know more about her without seeming too pushy.

Once dinner was over, they continued working until Ryder finally accepted the quote with a couple of modifications regarding the timeline.

Seraphina was exhausted and in a lot of pain, and ready to return to her suite for a hot bath to try and loosen her tight muscles before sleep. She noted it was very late and wondered how long it would take the car service to come and get her.

Ryder helped her out of her chair, quietly noting the pain etched on her face, helped her pack up her belongings, and took her briefcase while leaving his stuff behind on his desk.

"Let's get you back to your hotel; I imagine you're tired by now," he said, ushering her out of his office.

"I am, but it is also expected, right? Clients expect results on time and on budget, and sometimes, resting and such will have to be pushed to the end of a project; I am quite used to it by now," she told him.

"You shouldn't have to work so hard," he said softly, walking close to her with his hand resting on her shoulder before moving it to her back to guide her to his vehicle. "Don't you have a whole complement of consultants and contractors to do the job for you?"

"I do; however, most are very specialized in what they do. This is my area of expertise and my company. I have poured everything into making this work, and I refuse to let anything negatively mark the company, which is why I prefer to do most of the leg work myself," she told him, feeling the heat of his body close to her and his hand gently caressing her back. "Where are you taking me Mr. Durand?" she asked, unconsciously moving closer to him.

"I am leading you to my vehicle so I can take you back to the hotel. I saw you arrive in a car service and at this time of night, who knows how long they will take to come and get you. It's just easier if I take you myself," he told her.

"Makes sense," she agreed as they arrived at his SUV. Ryder helped her into his car before going around to the driver side to get in. "Thank you for driving me back, I appreciate it."

"Of course; I love to drive, and you get to where you need. Its win–win I would say," he told her, trying to concentrate on the road and not on the beautiful woman beside him.

She softly laughed at his comment, "I imagine driving is in your soul," she said.

"That it is, I grew up around racetracks; shaped me and my attitudes into the person I am today," he told her. "But I'm also smart enough to know when to step back and let experts do their jobs. Its why I've decided to retire at the end of the upcoming season, it's time to let the young ones strut their stuff."

"You're retiring? Wow, I hadn't heard that," she said, surprised.

"Yea, I'm not getting any younger, and it's harder to stay in shape and out of trouble. Besides, this company has been taking most of my attention these days," he admitted.

"That is very mature of you to know when it's time to move on," she said, thinking of her own changes she had made.

"Yep, now if only I could find that special someone to make my life complete," he said before he realized he had said that.

"Don't we all want that?" she agreed, hearing the wistfulness in his voice. "Maybe one day I will settle down enough to find someone. At my age though, I think I missed my opportunity."

"I don't believe that; you have to be what, thirty at the most?" he asked, surprised.

"Ha-ha, thank you for the compliment. I'm forty," she said with a laugh, seeing the look on his face.

"Get out, I don't believe you!" he exclaimed as they pulled into the hotel valet parking.

"Seriously, I turned forty a little while ago. Thank you, Ryder, have yourself a good evening. I will let you know when we will flood your company with people," she said as she went to gather her things.

"Hang on, allow me," he said, parking the car, getting out, and coming around to her side to help her out.

"Quite the gentleman," she murmured.

"I have to be, or my mother would have my ears," he told her as she accepted his hand from her seat.

"Ah, I see; your mother raised you right. That is good; so many have lost those gentlemanly values," she said, noting that he still had her hand and was walking with her into the hotel.

She had a bout of nervousness of what to do. 'Do I pull my hand away, or do I just leave it thinking he forgot he was holding my hand?' she thought to herself.

Together they stopped at the elevator, and quietly waited for the doors to open. Once opened, he ushered her into the elevator and waited for her to press her floor. Her thoughts were solely on him; his bad boy vibe was showing less and less, and what she was seeing was a very gentle and kind man. Through her short time with him so far, she learned he had a quick sense of humor, and he had a very serious side too. How he was so focused on work was not lost on her as he made sure his employee's needs would still be met with the changes. And he wanted a family.

Now she was feeling a little awkward as he still had her hand, and she had no idea what to do. The doors opened on her floor, and he waited for her to take the lead, following a step behind her to her room.

Once she opened the door, he let go of her hand and placed her briefcase down on a nearby chair. "Nice suite," he commented as he helped her out of her coat and placed it on the same chair as her briefcase.

"It works for me. Thank you for bringing me safely to my room," she murmured as he walked towards her.

"Of course, I must make sure you stay safe, you are worth millions to me, and I cannot let anything happen to you," he replied as he took a step forward, and gently placed his lips on hers.

She stood there feeling shocked for a moment before she realized that she was responding to his kiss and feeling her body heat from his gentle touches.

Once he broke the kiss, he looked into her eyes, and saw the war within, "I am sorry for being too forward. You are the most beautiful woman I have ever laid eyes on, and you're someone I want to get to know better," he said, again taking her hand into his, hoping she understood; he didn't want a fling this time around.

"I am so sorry Ryder; I am, especially if I made any untoward signals to you. I cannot date clients as it creates a rather large conflict of interest," she told him, hoping he understood that for her, the job would always come first.

"Really? Not even one small exception? Please Seraphina, let me in," he whispered against her lips, desperately wanting her to say 'yes' to him before capturing her lips in another sweet yet hot kiss before sweeping her up into his arms.

Chapter 8

*V*ery early the next morning, Seraphina woke feeling like she had run a marathon. "Crap," she mumbled under her breath. She moved her head and looked at the time, "Double crap, who the hell thought a meeting this early was a good idea anyways?"

She got up and went to get ready for the day; thinking about her dreams during the night and how erotic they were, and especially who they were with. She emerged from her bedroom into the sitting room to see the two tables laden with documents, waiting for her attention. She had an instant and overwhelming sensation course through her, making her shiver. "Ah shit," she muttered at the knock on her door, happy for the distraction.

She opened the door to find Ryder standing there with coffee and something that smelled good. "God isn't this too early for you?" she asked, letting him in, surprised he was awake already.

"Ha-ha, I can get up early when I have to; it's not that I like it or anything, but here I am." Ryder said, setting down coffee and breakfast on the table. "So, how much free time do you have before crazy sets in?" he asked, giving her the breakfast sandwich.

"I have no time; as of this morning, we kick into high gear," she replied, before taking a bite.

"I was hoping to show you around and such today," Ryder said, disappointed.

"I'm so sorry about that, but I'm on the clock and I have a year's worth of work to get done in a very small amount of time," she told him.

Ryder looked at her, and noted what she was wearing, "You are beautiful," he said.

She smiled at him, "Thank you, and now I have to kick you out, I have so much work do to for two clients, with you being one of them, and I am now on an impossibly tight timeline to get my work done," she said.

"You have to go Ryder, seriously," she told him, after they had finished breakfast, and noted he was trying to stall.

Her attempts of trying to make him understand that she was in no position to start a fling, or a relationship, or anything, had been muted by his kisses. She had to admit, he was an amazing kisser, and she could not help herself. It had been at least ten, no, maybe fifteen years since anyone had touched her. Her judgment had been colored by her baser desires and had let Ryder stay far too long in her room, kissing. She had finally put a stop to their make out session when she felt too close to her own breaking point, wanting way too much from him, but also not allowing herself to cross that line.

He got up and moved towards the door, "Yea, I get that you're all about work," Ryder said, feeling disappointed.

"I am especially now; you have to understand. I am sorry if I led you on, but I can't start anything with you or anyone," she told him softly.

"I do understand, I was just hoping that you would let me be the exception," he told her, gathering her into his arms. "I am developing feelings for you, and I want to see where this goes."

"Ryder, I can't, I'm sorry," she told him, before gently breaking from his embrace to open the door to her suite. "Have a good day," she told him softly as he left.

Once she had the door closed, she leaned against it, "Holy hell," she said to herself, "maybe I need a one-night stand or something so I can get my head on straight."

Seraphina and Grant spent the day getting all the details in place to literally move three-quarters of her company to North Carolina quickly. They were on a super tight timeline, and both were busy securing workspaces and signing the leases that they had placed a hold on the day before. Grant would be flying out that evening to meet up with Seraphina to begin the arduous task of getting one workspace set, while she worked on the other. The rest of their crew would arrive in the next couple of days; however, the teams were already working on their assigned client.

"Jesus, are we stupid, or is it me who is beyond stupid to think we could do both at the same time?" she asked Grant, during one of their many video calls that day.

"You aren't stupid; I too thought we could do both at the same time, or I would have drawn up one quote and made sure the other one stayed on the back burner until we could properly handle them," he grumbled. "We can do this, it's just hard right now because we are essentially dividing the company into two for a few months. Upside is we're all going to be in the same city; the downside is the two work sites aren't side by side."

"We were lucky to get the two sites we did; they're big enough for what we will need, and have everything we require to ensure our staff, consultants, and contractors are comfortable while they are working," she replied. "And they are in proximity to the clients' campuses so the travel will be a minimum, which will save time there."

Grant sighed, "Yea, I know. Kelley is a little grumpy that I'm deploying again so soon. She wanted us to work on that baby she wanted," he said softly.

"Tell Kelley that she can come see you any time she has a break; I am sure you two can find some time somewhere to make a baby," she replied, "besides, she knows how this business is and she really isn't all that grumpy. I talked to her this morning, and she was complaining how you were getting underfoot already. I think she's just missing your body, not you per se," she said with a giggle.

"Funny," Grant grumbled. "I'm already driving her nuts, eh? I kind of figured as much; she and Kayla have everything down to the minute regarding their schedules and every time I'm home, I throw the monkey wrench into the works."

"Well, I wouldn't say nuts already, it's just you do throw their schedules off kilter. I never figured out how you and Kelley have managed to stay married for so long and not have the issues so many of our other friends had," she said as she signed yet another contract regarding catering for her company.

"Yea, me neither. She seems to love me no matter what, so, I'm lucky to have her," Grant confirmed.

"One day I may get lucky, but I'm not going to hold my breath; I think I missed my window of opportunity," she replied distractedly, thinking back to Ryder and his comment about wanting to get to know her.

"You never know Sera. I don't think you missed your window, but you've been too busy working instead of enjoying life like other people. You frankly aren't looking and have missed a few men who've been plainly trying to gain your attention," he told her as he double checked the flights, making sure he didn't miss anyone.

"No one has been looking at me, or trying to get my attention," she protested.

"You keep telling yourself that, and you really will have missed that window of opportunity," Grant told her. "Ok, all the flights are booked, as are the hotel rooms."

"Good; the workspaces and food are booked, and all of the materials and electronics are already on the way here; tomorrow will be the start of complete chaos," she said, thinking, "I'm not missing anything, am I?"

"Just travel to and from the work sites and hotels," Grant said.

"Nope, that's already been taken care of. We have those fifteen passenger vans booked to run as shuttles for us; luckily, the hotels we're all in are within a three-square block radius, so walking between hotels will not be an issue," she confirmed.

"Then, I think we have everything; I will see you tomorrow morning, I don't get in until super late, so I won't bother you until tomorrow morning," he told her.

"Perfect; safe travels, and I'll see you tomorrow morning," she said before she hung up.

Chapter 9

Seraphina woke up with a killer headache, "What the hell?" she muttered as she looked at the time and heard the storm. "Great, its only ten, and there's a hell of a storm."

She got up and went to take her medication before going to the window to look out and see what the storm was doing. She watched for a few minutes before hearing her phone indicate a message.

She retrieved her phone, seeing it was Grant and called him back, "Let me guess, you're stranded somewhere," she said, not even saying hello.

"How'd you guess?" Grant asked, sounding surprised.

"There's a hell of a storm here; it woke me up and gave me one hell of an awesome headache," she told him, going back to the window. "So, where are you stuck?"

"I'm stuck in New York; apparently, there's the remnants of a hurricane where you are, wreaking havoc on everything," he replied.

"That would be about right," she said softly, still watching the storm from her window.

"That good huh? So, I have no idea when I will get in; they are saying maybe another 48 to 72 hours or so," he told her.

"Ah shit; that's not good. Well, it cannot be helped, I guess. We can't control the weather," she said, going to sit on the sofa.

"Well, look at it this way; this will give you a day or so of down time before the madness sets in; use this time to recharge a bit, enjoy dinner and some pampering," Grant said, giving her what he hoped would be something she would like.

"That sounds good; there are some people who want to go for dinner and such, and spending some time getting my back rested won't hurt either," she said, thinking.

"Exactly, use the time. Maybe this is God's way of making you slow down a bit," he told her gently.

"Funny," she muttered. "Shit! Well, until all this crap clears up and everyone is down here, we are in a holding pattern. I will let the clients know that due to weather we have our first delay."

"They know the weather can't be controlled, and I'm sure they will understand," he said.

"Yea, I agree. If they could control weather; they would never have rain delays," she said with a laugh. "Ok; get yourself a nice hotel room and hunker down until this system is gone, I guess."

"I'm already on the way to the hotel now, and I will shoot you the information when I get there, and I will let Kelley know what happened, so she doesn't worry," he said.

"Perfect; she does seem to worry about your ass for some unknown reason," Seraphina muttered, rubbing her hurting head.

"It's because I make her happy if you get my drift," he said teasingly.

"Yuck, that's like knowing about your parent's sex life, no thank you. I'm hanging up now, hoping to get some sleep here. Have fun in New York," she said before she hung up with Grant laughing in her ear.

She sat back and thought about this new development. Her normal contingency plans did not include delays due to weather. "Well hell; this is a new one for us," she muttered, thinking, "literally nothing I can do until everyone gets here and who knows when that will be," she said, grabbing the remote and turning on the TV to the weather channel.

"Holy shit, this is a hell of a storm," she mumbled after a few minutes, seeing the forecast for the next several days. "Great, no one's getting here on time."

She grabbed her phone and sent a note to Grant that all the flights will have to be changed. He replied that he was already on it. "Of course, he's already on it; he's another version of you," she said, rubbing her face wishing her headache would ease a little bit.

She watched the reports for a little while longer, paying close attention to the radar. "Fuck," she mumbled, hearing her phone indicate a message.

Figuring it was Grant, she looked and was a little surprised to see it was from Ryder, "Great."

She called him back, and he picked up on the first ring. "Evening Ryder, I am fine, thank you. Yes, this storm woke me up and I am having a delightful time with the headache that popped in for shits and giggles. No, I don't need someone to come and scare away the boogey man or whatever storm monster pops out with these storms, I have experience dealing with them myself," she said in one breath.

Ryder took a moment before laughing, "Okay; I get you're fine, and I also know that Seattle normally doesn't get storms like these and I wondered how you were doing with this one," he said, more seriously.

She laughed, "I'm fine really, I have a killer headache that isn't going away even though I have taken my medication. My right-hand, Grant is grounded in New York for now, and the rest of my team his back in Seattle. God knows when we will get everyone here to start on the project, so I hate to say this; I'm sorry Ryder, but there's a delay in our start date," she said professionally at the end.

"You can't control the weather and it's still hurricane season in this part of the continent, and sometimes the storms are hell," he replied.

"Good thing you understand. This is our first delay due to weather; I have contingency plans for just about everything else," she said, getting comfortable on the sofa.

"Well, sometimes you just have to go with it, right? So, with this delay, what are you going to do?" he asked.

"I have no idea; I have never had time like this to myself. Grant suggested that I pamper myself a bit and rest," she replied.

"Those are good ideas for sure; I'm sure you need the rest, and sometimes getting pampered is a good thing too," he agreed, "we could go for dinner too; it's not like you don't have time and hey, you have to eat."

"True, I do. Sure, we can go to dinner," she agreed.

Ryder felt his heart leap for joy, "Awesome, how about tomorrow evening? I know this cool little place that has amazing food."

"Sounds great to me, I will see you tomorrow Ryder, good night," she said as she hung up the phone.

"Might as well, it's not like you don't have the time, and you haven't officially started the project yet," she said to herself, turning the TV off as she got up from the sofa and went to her bedroom, "Ok, time to try and get some sleep; headache, please go away."

Chapter 10

Seraphina spent the morning working with her teams, discussing some potential ways to get back on track once everyone finally hit the ground. Once that was done, she went to the hotel's spa where she had an appointment for a manicure and pedicure, a facial and a body salt scrub. She had managed to get some sleep and even slept in a bit to make up for the late night. Her head was still pounding though, and figured that with the storm, it would not be going anywhere anytime soon and thought some other therapies might help.

As she was waiting for her name to be called for her spa treatments, she heard her phone, and saw that Jason was calling her. "Hi Jason, how are you on this wonderful and stormy day?" She said, trying to sound super cheerful.

"Hi Seraphina, you alright?" He asked, wondering what would make her so happy in this storm.

"I am doing fine Jason, thank you. Due to the delay, there's not much I can do, so I am pampering myself this afternoon," she said, sounding more like herself.

"That's great, some down time will be good before all hell breaks loose here," he said, having heard about the timeline and what Mr. B wanted.

"That is putting it mildly, and yes, it is good. I don't get a lot of down time and decided to take advantage while I can. So, some pampering and rest is on the docket until this stupid storm dissipates or moves somewhere else," she said.

"Cool, so I was wondering about that dinner you agreed with me," Jason said.

"Right, I did agree to dinner with you; well, its Sunday and I have something planned for this evening, and I have some other things booked in, so how about Friday evening then?" she replied, thinking.

"I think that will be perfect; I will pick you up at seven," Jason confirmed, feeling happy she kept her agreement to dinner with him.

Seraphina hung up and had just put her phone away when she heard her named being called, "Yay, me time," she said to herself, feeling excited.

Seraphina heard the knock on the door and knew it was Ryder; she opened the door to find him in a polo shirt and clean jeans. Knowing his preference for casual, she had dressed in a similar fashion.

Ryder stood there, drinking in her beauty, "Wow, you are beautiful," he said, taking in her glowing skin.

"Thank you, it's amazing what a facial and salt scrub can do," she replied, letting him into her suite.

"Nope, its more than that; you're glowing, like you got some rest and feeling good for a change," he said, beginning to understand her workaholic tendencies.

"Why, thank you Mr. Durand; I did manage a nap after my spa session, and I am feeling good; even that blasted headache has lessened, I'm hoping it will go away for good soon," she said, putting on her coat.

"Where are we going?" She asked, as he escorted her from her suite.

"There's this little place that has amazing food; it's got all kinds of home cooking and stick to your ribs kind of food. It's like a mom and pops type shop, very comfortable and laid back," he told her, resting his hand on her back, feeling the muscles. "Your muscles aren't as tight as before, that has to be good."

"It is good; I have another treatment booked tomorrow for massage and acupuncture; I find that's what helps the most when my muscles decide to seize up, and my drug regime can really do the trick too, if I can catch it on time," she told him as he continued to caress her back.

That to her felt amazing; having someone caress her like they cared. Gentle touches and such she had not felt in years. This was beginning to cause conflict within herself. Ryder was her client, yet on the other hand, she wanted what she thought he was offering.

They quietly drove to the restaurant, each lost in their own thoughts. When they arrived, Ryder quickly got out, grabbing the umbrella and going to the passenger side to help Seraphina from his vehicle.

Once inside, Seraphina looked about and saw that even though the weather was horrible, the place was filled with people, "It must be a good spot if people come out in this weather," she said.

"It is just wait," he replied quietly.

They were shown to a booth and given menus and water. After a few minutes, "Wow, look at the choices here; most I have no idea about. It's mostly staple and comfort food in these parts, right?" she asked Ryder.

"It is but there are other options that aren't southern," he said, showing her the area.

"Cool, too many choices I think," she said to herself. "I still have no idea what I want though."

An older lady with her hair tied back in a bun came to their table, "Well, I'll be, Ryder finally brought a lady! Good evening, I'm Mom, and this young'un comes in here every week promising me he will bring in a lady. I honestly thought I was going to my grave before this troublemaker made good on his promise," she said in her southern accent, as she pinched Ryder's cheeks.

Seraphina laughed, "Well, he made good on one promise, tell me, what should I have?" she asked Mom.

"Oh honey, you ain't from 'round here, are ya?" Mom asked.

"Nope, Seattle; please, help?" she asked as Mom gave a pretend hurt look at hearing where Seraphina was from before saying, "I know exactly what you two need to have on a night like this." she said, taking their menus and walking away from their table.

"She's awesome," she said to Ryder, whose cheeks were still a little pink.

"She is even if she tries hard to embarrass me," Ryder admitted. "I do come in here at least once a week; sometimes with a few buddies, and sometimes alone. She has been bugging me that I'm not getting any younger and that I should look for a lady to settle down with. Now that I'm in my forties, it's something that I don't really think about anymore."

"Ah, yea, like me; I think I missed my window, and concluded that I will be single. I'm good with that now, but for a bit, I think I might have been a little heartbroken about it," she said, understanding how he felt.

"You understand; things don't always happen when you want them to; God knows I've tried with a few relationships, but my partners hated that I was away a lot, or I was always working and stuff. They wanted me to focus on them only. I don't know, maybe I was looking in the wrong places, but I enjoy being the fun uncle, and when I need a kid fix; there are those close to me who have kids and will let me spend time with them," he said.

"Exactly, my best friends, Kelley and Grant have a daughter that I have helped raise, and Kelley desperately wants another baby before she thinks it's too late. I too get my fix from Kayla; she and I have a bond and we do stuff that is just for us, and her parents completely dote on her," Seraphina told him quietly.

"Yup, sounds a lot like me; we have other things that we now focus on, and we're happy," he agreed, not wanting her to see his face and how much he still wanted a family.

"There are days when I still want it all: a loving husband, kids, work, life, fun and such," she said wistfully, not realizing she said that louder than intended. Ryder heard, and knew that she wanted exactly what he wanted, and decided that he would be the one to give her the whole package.

Chapter 11

*L*ater that evening, having been stuffed with some of the best food Seraphina ever had, they returned to her suite for a nightcap, and to continue with their conversation.

She learned that Ryder loved owning a racing company and racing as an entire sport. He loved the outdoors, preferring to fish when he had the time. He also owned a house out in the woods of Maine that he would retreat to when he needed a break from city life. She had been seeing a side to Ryder that he had not shown to others. She knew of his reputation in the racing scene, but this Ryder was different. He was every inch the gentleman, making sure everyone else's needs were taken care of before his own. He made sure to say good night to Mom with a hug before leaving the restaurant.

"I can barely move," she mumbled.

"Yup, Mom fed you really good; she must have thought that you don't eat enough," Ryder replied with amusement.

"Well, after everything she placed in front of me, I won't need to eat until next week sometime. She just kept bringing us stuff, and that hot bread pudding was amazing," she replied.

"Yup, it is and one of my favorites too," he replied, taking a sip from his drink.

"Tonight, has been so much fun Seraphina, thank you for making this evening memorable," he said after a few minutes.

"Thank you for an amazing dinner; I had a lot of fun this evening too," she replied, also taking a sip from her drink.

Ryder got to know more about her; how her brain worked. She loved racing as he learned and had gotten into it purely by chance; she was bored one Sunday afternoon and came across it as she was flipping through the channels looking for something to watch. Since then, she was hooked.

He wondered why he hadn't seen her at any races as she admitted that she tried to go to two per season, dependent on her schedule. He also found out that her best friends had been with her for many years, having worked together for most of their adult life.

"So, what got you into consulting work?" he asked, scooting next to where she was sitting.

"I needed a career change, and I worked for a few different consulting firms, learning what they did and such. I also realized that the companies I worked for did not do a thorough job like I preferred, and after some soul searching, decided to start my own consulting business. I had been told by a few ex-bosses that I would never be good enough to consult on my own, and now, I'm sometimes hired to clean up after those companies, ah, I love karma," she told him, shifting to lean into him.

"Really? That is so cool; so, what did you do before consulting?" Ryder asked as he casually placed his arm behind her head and rested it on her shoulders, bringing her closer.

"I used to work for the government doing international relations," she told him, hoping he would drop the subject.

"So, you traveled and did what the government told you to do?" he asked.

"Pretty much, and why I decided on a career change," she said, taking a sip, before putting her glass on the table. "I needed the change."

"I can understand that; a person can do so much before they get fed up, and I have heard that government jobs can be the worst when it comes to conflicting orders and such," he said as he also put his glass down.

"So, what do you see in your future?" he asked, wanting to know as much about her as possible.

"I'm not really sure; I have my business, and I hope to do this for as long as I can. After that, I have not made any concrete plans or really thought about it," she told him.

"You must have some dreams and wishes," he asked.

"Not really; most of what I wanted I have. I've made a name for myself and have a successful company. I have a beautiful house that is perfect for me, and it's not one of those large ego type ones, just big enough for me. And, I have a handful of true friends that I can count on for anything I may need," she said as she finished her glass.

Ryder got up and went to get the bottle they were drinking from to refill her glass. She did not refuse the refill, finding that she really was enjoying spending time with him.

"So, no dreams to travel, see some warm sandy beaches or take cruises as you please?" he asked.

"Not really; I might in the future, that stuff hasn't been on my bucket list," she replied.

"What about relationships?" he prompted after several minutes of silence, wanting to know of her past lovers.

"I don't have time for them, and you already know this; I have been focusing solely on my business," she replied, again draining her glass.

"Hmm," Ryder thought out loud.

They sat there for a while, not really saying anything important. Ryder had managed to refill their glasses a few more times as they talked. Seraphina, not being much of a drinker, was well on her way to inebriation. "I just don't know," she murmured to herself.

"Huh?" Ryder asked, not really hearing her.

"Just wondering if I should sleep with you, or put myself to bed," she murmured.

"Are you really considering this?" he asked, hopeful and surprised.

"You have featured in several of my dreams over the years. I would like to find out if you really are as good as you are in my dreams," she said as she stood and swayed ever so slightly. "Come with me," she said, taking his hand and leading Ryder to her bedroom.

There, she turned to face him, as he gently reached out to cup her face so he could kiss her. After several minutes of heated kissing, Ryder felt her hand slide underneath his shirt. "Are you sure Seraphina?" he asked, wanting to make sure she wanted this.

"Oh yea, I do," she replied as she reached for her own shirt, taking it off in one swoop.

"You are so beautiful Seraphina," he said softly, taking in her soft curves and glowing skin, before gently taking her hands and caressing her soft skin.

"Thank you," she murmured, loving the sensations of warm hands caressing her skin, leaving a hot trail where the hands moved.

Their hands roamed over each other, taking in the feel of their skin as each piece of clothing eventually found its way to the floor. When they found the bed, both were free of their clothing, and in need of something they could not explain.

Seraphina wanted to explore his body, and Ryder wanted to do the same, causing a bit of giggling between them. "Jesus, let me go first," she said, after they calmed their giggles.

She wanted to feel his skin against hers and wanted to see what she could do to bring him immense pleasure. She caressed him as her mouth licked and kissed all along his body before deciding to settle on his manhood; hard, with incredibly soft skin and a pulsing that begged attention.

She loved that her soft touches caused Ryder to quietly moan as his eyes rolled into his head as his lids closed tightly. She watched his face as she moved about his body, and she watched him very carefully as she took him into her mouth sliding her tongue along that very firm pulsing vein as she did.

Ryder was not expecting these sensations and when he felt her engulf him, he very nearly came. He could not control his body as it jerked, and his voice responded to the sensation with a loud cry of joy.

Seraphina concentrated on her movements, hearing his voice, and feeling his body vibrate with the building sensations.

"Please, Seraphina," he quietly begged, "please babe, stop, I'm so close," he rasped as she worked a little harder.

Ryder felt his eyes roll very far into the back of his head, his body took over and he was no longer in control as he came hard. When he floated back towards the bed, he became aware that she was still sucking and playing with his body.

"Oh god, please Seraphina, you need to stop," he begged as he tried to find the strength to physically stop her.

When he finally opened his eyes, he saw that she had fun. "You like bringing a man to his literal knees, do you?" he murmured.

"You are so much fun, Ryder," she replied quietly. She did have a lot of fun bringing him to his climax the way she had. She loved that he had let his body go, and not demand he remain in control.

"Please darling, you have to let me give you the same pleasure," he said to her as he found the strength to move, so that she was laying on the bed, and he could have his turn to explore her body more in-depth.

"I want you to know, this is so much more than just sex for me; my feelings for you are growing by the minute," he told her very softly as he started his exploration.

"I know Ryder," she murmured quietly, "you have a special place in my heart."

With that said, he started with his soft caresses of her incredibly soft skin. He noted that her skin was glowing, even though she had some scars from something that he did not know about. Ryder figured that she was normally conscious of these very scars, the ones that he was kissing, while creating gentle shivers as she was caught up in the web of love they were creating together. He made sure to kiss every single scar, seeing them along her back, buttocks, and upper legs. While he kissed and caressed, he also studied them, and seeing a pattern, knew these were not good scars upon her body.

Seraphina was taking in every caress and kiss that Ryder bestowed upon her body. She felt loved, cherished, and desired; it was something that she had not experienced, and it was like a drug to her, wanting more and more.

He made sure to bring her the sensations her body was craving by her responses to his touches. When he eventually found her most feminine place, he paid homage. Gentle kisses, licks, and nips; he wanted to bring her to a place of pure ecstasy.

He heard her moans and mews as he worked, and knew she was close by the growing tremors of her body. He heard her cries and watched her face closely as he guided her body over the edge, into a place he did not know that she had never been before. He watched as her body instantly flushed as she thrashed about as his mouth and hands worked her body, as only an expert could.

Ryder slowed his movements, bringing more gentle caresses and kisses as he waited for her to come back to earth. He wanted her to feel his feelings for her; knowing how much he was smitten with her; and how much he wanted to pursue a real relationship with her. As far as he was concerned, he was done with the flings and one-night stands.

Chapter 12

Very early the next morning, Ryder had a call from one of his race teams; they had an issue that needed his immediate attention. As much as he wanted to wake Seraphina up and let her know he had to leave; he thought it better that she get some quality sleep as they had not slept much during the night, preferring to explore each other and make love several times.

Ryder quietly left her suite; hoping he had not pushed her into a direction she was not ready for, yet praying to God that she was feeling the same way, and wanted the same things that he did; love, family, and that connection that made people love each other on a level only the heavens knew of.

Before he left; he kissed her gently on her forehead, "I am in love with you Seraphina, please God, let me into her heart and soul as I know now that she and I were made for each other," he whispered, taking in her peaceful slumber.

Later that morning, Seraphina woke feeling very groggy. That was normal for her if she had taken her medication and figured the previous night's dreams were her normal ones of a man she knew she could never have, yet continued to dream about. "I really need to let this go," she whispered to herself, thinking about her dreams of her and Ryder making love together.

Once her cobwebs were somewhat cleared from her brain, she got up to get ready for the day. She had a massage and acupuncture booked for her back; she hoped that she had gotten over this episode of pain so she could concentrate on her two clients. She also had a conference call with her teams, to see where everyone was at and what would be needed once everyone finally hit the ground.

As she climbed out of bed, she noted her headache was gone as was most of her aches and pains. She went to look out the window and saw grey skies with more rain. She noted the rain was not as heavy as the day before. "I wonder when the tail of this storm will show up," she murmured to herself as she turned on the TV to see what the weather had in store for today.

While she watched, her mind returned to her dreams of Ryder and the immense pleasure they brought each other, "Heavens, those dreams seemed so real," she whispered as her brain replayed the events. "So real that I can feel his touch on my body and smell his cologne," she said, hugging herself.

After a while, she turned off the TV, knowing she was no longer paying any attention and decided to shower and get started for her day ahead. "Once everyone is here, there won't be time for anything," she murmured.

While she was waiting for her treatment, she saw Jason walk in, "Well, hello you," she said to him as he sat next to her.

"Hello yourself; how are you doing?" he asked.

"Not too bad actually; my body is beginning to behave, so, I am hoping after this treatment, I will be back to my normal self," she told him.

"Cool, I imagine that will be good for you to concentrate on your work," he said to her.

"Yes, it will be, and I find life in general is better for me," she replied, "what about you? Do you find these treatments to be helpful?"

"I do; I had some issues awhile back and a close friend mentioned that having regular massages and therapy would help me to maintain my flexibility and movements," Jason told her.

"That it can if you can catch it early enough," she agreed, "unfortunately for me, I was not as quick, so it's more maintenance than preventative."

"Ah, for you it's to help you prevent severe pain," he realized.

"Yup; some days, my body really hates me, and any movement can be incredibly difficult for me," she admitted. "I hate it of course, but it is what it is. I can't change it, only manage, so it's what I try to do so I don't wind up being one of those super grumpy people."

"I can't see you being grumpy," Jason replied with a snicker.

Seraphina laughed, "Ask my team that question, I know they have some stories that are doozies of me being grumpy," she told him as her name was called. "I will see you Friday evening Jason; have a good one," she said as she left to follow her therapist.

Seraphina left her treatment session feeling pretty good considering. She returned to her suite for a nap before her conference call that evening.

While she napped, her dreams featured that one man, the one who could fulfill her every need, and was unattainable. When she woke, "Dammit! I can't even have a decent nap without him disturbing my dreams!" she grumbled as she decided to forgo the remainder of her planned nap and get up to try and focus on something other than Ryder Durand.

Her conference call that evening was exactly what she thought it would be; the team were very efficient and had been working diligently on their respective clients even if they could not be in North Carolina to properly interact and begin analyzing the client they were assigned to.

"Everything seems so easy with the team," she mentioned to Grant that evening. He was to fly out Thursday evening to begin the crazy of working two clients at the same time while keeping each piece of information with the appropriate client.

"Shit, this could go sideways if we fuck up what goes with which client," he mentioned thoughtfully, "we're going to need a fail-safe for these two clients, just in case."

"I was thinking that; maybe color code the clients and see how that goes?" she replied, writing a few notes while she talked.

"Maybe; but it's also the other stuff, right? Sure, some documents and such we can color code, but it's also the research and non-tangibles that we will need to figure out," Grant told her.

"Crap, I have no idea at the moment. It's bad enough my brain has been seriously misbehaving," she muttered.

"Bad brain, how is that possible?" he asked curiously.

"For the past couple of days, a certain person has been front and center in some incredibly vivid dreams, and no matter how hard I've been trying, I can't get them to stop," she told him, knowing he would likely tease her.

"Oh? Nice! You need a man you know, if anything, just to get some good sex," he started, "besides, I'm sure you'd have no problem getting Ryder into your bed."

"I did not mention names Grant," she chastised, hearing him laugh.

"I know, and I know you. Ryder would be the man you want to have some fun with. So, go for it, have that fun," he told her.

"You know I can't! That would create quite the conflict of interest, wouldn't you say?" she reminded him.

"Hey, we haven't started yet; you have a window, use it." Grant told her before he hung up.

"Dammit; I just can't win," she muttered, "that one night stand is sounding better, but there's no way, I'd let some guy touch me."

Chapter 13

Seraphina was just putting the finishing touches on her make-up, not that she wore a lot, but sometimes she wanted to feel pretty. She looked at herself and determined she was ready for dinner with Jason. While she waited for Jason, she thought back to what Grant mentioned to her a few times before. Did she miss opportunities to have relationships? Were there men who were interested in her, and tried to gain her attention? Well, Ryder was one who expressed an interest in her; then again, he was also known as a player in the racing world.

"God, I don't have time to have a relationship! I have so much work on my plate and a huge time crunch that is about to become my life. I need to focus on my job, and just put the rest of my life back on the shelf until I do have time to deal with it," she said to no one in particular, feeling that unrest she felt when she didn't have any work for her to fill her time. "What am I even doing going to dinner tonight? I should be working getting ready for the onslaught of work that is going to hit my desk in no time."

Just then, there was a call on the suite phone. It was the main desk telling her that Jason had arrived and was now waiting for her. She grabbed her coat, cane, and purse, before leaving her suite, "Ok kiddo, this is just dinner; nothing more can happen, right?" she told herself in the elevator. "Listen body, we are not having sex any time soon, so just put that shit away."

As soon as the elevator doors opened, she saw Jason patiently waiting for her. As soon as he saw her, his face broke out into a grin which made her heart leap.

"You are incredibly beautiful," Jason said as he gathered her in for a hug. "And you smell so good too."

"Thank you, Jason, you are looking quite dashing yourself," she replied, taking in his perfectly pressed suit, minus the tie. "I don't recall seeing you in a suit before."

"Sometimes I need the suit; meetings with potential sponsors, potential partners and such," he told her as he turned, and placed her hand on his arm to guide her from the lobby.

"Ah, yes, I can see that. Having a few good suits should be in every man's closet," she replied as he led her to his SUV.

Once she was settled into the passenger seat, Jason got into his own seat, "How was today?" he asked as he started the vehicle and pulled out onto the street.

"It was busy; I think we are ready to start the project and I hope we can keep the timeline too. Tomorrow, I will have consultants and my right-hand here and things will definitely kick into very high gear," she told him as she passively watched the scenery pass.

"That's great; I'm sure you will do an amazing job," Jason replied.

"For you? Yes, it is great; you will see some changes that should help you and your team in the long run. I hope that you and the other team members will be open to what we propose for changes," she said.

"I'm sure there might be some grumbling, and most of that grumbling will be from me, sorry in advance by the way. I know we need to make changes; we cannot keep operating the way we have been. My budget for the last few years is one number, but my actual expenses are a completely different number, and I know that's not good for the company," Jason said.

"Well, knowing that is a great start, thank you, and I will take your advance apology and ensure whichever consultant or contractor knows you have already apologized," she said.

"Thanks, I know I'm not an easy person to work with. I have been called a perfectionist, too focused, too stringent, too single minded. I've heard it all; I even heard that I sleep with my clipboard," he said, laughing, "It's who I am, and well, I'm not going to apologize for that. It's gotten me some championships so far, so I'd say I'm doing something right."

Seraphina laughed as well, "I have heard the same about me minus the clipboard part. I know I am focused and goal oriented. It's why my company is so successful, and why companies like Brandon Motorsports seek me out to help them," she agreed.

Jason pulled into the valet parking of a high-end restaurant, "Jason, wow, look at this place! You didn't have to bring me to a place like this," she told him, impressed with the restaurant he had chosen for dinner.

"No: a beautiful woman like you deserves a place like this. You should be pampered and showered with beauty, like you," he said as he pulled her in close to him. "You are the most beautiful woman I have ever seen; I feel blessed that you agreed to dinner with me, granted as friends, but I would like us to become more if you'll grant me that privilege," he said very softly to her, looking deeply into her eyes.

Seraphina felt a connection with Jason; one she was very tempted to explore yet knew she could not. "Oh Jason, as much as I would like to explore this, I can't; I've been hired by your employer to do a job," she said just as quietly.

"Exactly how much work will you be doing on this project?" he asked as they waited for their table, pulling her as close as he dared.

"I will be guiding all of my consultants and contractors through every step, and I will be presenting Mr. Brandon with the final set of recommendations to him once this project is completed; I can't at this time. Maybe in another time and world we are meant to be, but here and now, I just can't," she gently pleaded with him.

"Seraphina, I will never place you in a position where you cannot do your job properly and feel you are being pushed by me. I would love to pursue whatever this is between us, but I know how important your job is, and why I suggested dinner as friends for now," he said, once they were settled at their table in a corner that was away from prying eyes.

"Thank you, Jason, that means a lot to me. I would love to have you as a friend, but I think we have already crossed that line," she said, looking deep into his eyes, seeing the gold specks dancing in the light.

Before anything more could be said, the wait staff ascended upon their table to take their drink and dinner orders, while placing a small basket of assorted freshly made buns and filling their water glasses. And just as quickly, they descended from sight.

"Holy hell, I don't think I've ever had service like that," she said, amused. "That was amazing!"

"I love this place simply because of their service. This place prides itself on the service they provide, and it is excellent," Jason told her as he took a sip from his water glass.

"I can imagine," she said, impressed with the restaurant so far. If the food turned out to be half as good, she would treat her company to this place before they headed home.

"Seraphina, I know you have that rule, and I get why you have it. It makes perfect sense to me; but here I am, having some very deep feelings for you already, ones I haven't felt in a long time, and I am fighting with myself because I don't want to put you in a place where you have to choose between me or work, but I also want to spend all of my time with you, learning everything I can about you," he said, taking her hand into his. "All I can do is hope and pray you feel the same, and maybe when you have completed your job with Brandon Motorsports, we can then pursue a deep and meaningful relationship," he said, placing all his cards on the table for her to see.

"Oh, Jason...," she started but was interrupted by the delivery of their meals and the bottle of wine that would complement their meal perfectly.

Once they were left alone, Seraphina had difficulty forming her words, "Jason, I just can't, and I don't know what the future will hold for me," she said gently.

Jason thought about her comment for a moment before responding, "You're scared, aren't you?" he asked thoughtfully.

She sighed as she thought, "I don't know if that's it, or if it's something else. I have not had a relationship in... god..., maybe ten or more years, I think? I've been focusing all of my energy on my company and being successful," she told him as they ate their dinner. "It's just something I've chosen not to think about really."

Jason took in her words, and realized she was indeed scared to open herself to anyone. "Seraphina, love can be an amazing ride; you need to open your heart to someone," he said as he moved his hand to caress her face. "Please think about this."

Seraphina was quiet for a little bit thinking about her life and the choices she had made. "I'm sure it is, but for me, I don't have that luxury." she said simply.

Chapter 14

Jason decided that the remainder of the evening to keep the topics of discussion light and easygoing. He got the message that she was not sure, and there was a war within her; something he wanted to put a stop to. Making her comfortable was his priority, and the remainder of dinner was that; comfortable and fun.

They talked about different subjects from favorite foods, to phobias, and what a perfect day consists of. Jason learned a lot about her; she loved spice, hated rodents, and a perfect day to her was a good book by a fire with a large cup of coffee or tea tucked under a cozy blanket in an oversized chair for her to curl up in.

She learned that he was very goal-oriented, loved to cook, and workout when he found the time. He also told her that he hadn't time for relationships either simply because he wanted to win another championship, and figured he needed to get that while he was still in the position of crew chief.

When dinner was finished, Jason offered they go for a drive so he could show her some of the sights. She was agreeable, thinking an evening with no work would help her before the storm that was brewing.

He led her to his SUV and helped her get in before tipping the valet and getting settled into his own seat. "There are some amazing sights to see around here I'd like to show you," he said as he drove out of the parking lot.

"Sure, that sounds great," she agreed.

They were quiet for a few minutes as he drove to an area that he thought would be perfect to see the city from.

When they arrived at the place, he parked so they could see the city from the car, but also left room in case she wanted to get out and walk for a bit. "What do you think of the view?" he asked her as he turned off the car.

"Wow, this is some view. You can see the whole city from here," she said, taking it all in.

"It's a very cool place to come and think or do nothing. There's also a lot of biking trails just behind us that go further up the hill," he said.

She took off her seat belt and made to get out of the SUV causing Jason to jump into action to help her from his car. Once she was out, she walked towards the fence, lining the edge of the hill. "Wow," was all she could say.

"Yea, the first time I came up here, I had the same reaction," he told her, coming up behind her.

"I love the sounds of the crickets, and night, and at the same time see the beauty of the city. What a combination," she said, feeling Jason just behind her.

She closed her eyes, taking in the sounds, and the scent of Jason's aftershave. She very slowly inhaled then exhaled, feeling her body respond to the closeness of his body. Just as she opened her eyes, she felt his arms go around her, pulling her closer to him, supporting her.

She leaned against him, neither saying anything, enjoying the view and the sounds of the night. They stood like that for an unknown amount of time. "Time stands still here," she said after a while.

"It does; how are your back and hips doing?" he asked, concerned.

"They are beginning to yell at me, so I'm thinking it's time for me to sit and let the muscles rest for a bit," she told him, moving from his embrace.

"Of course, let's get you back to your room so you can rest," he said gently, taking her over to the passenger side of the SUV, and helping her get in. "God, help me," he muttered to himself as he walked around the back of his vehicle, "I'm in too deep already."

The drive back to the hotel was a comfortable quiet, each lost in their thoughts, half listening to the radio that was turned low. When they arrived at the hotel, Jason parked the car and gave the valet his keys before going to her side of the car to help her out, offering her his hand.

As they walked into the lobby, Jason had pulled her close to him, almost like protecting her, while guiding her to the elevator. While they waited, Jason pulled her a little closer and brushed his lips against her temple, "You truly are amazing, thank you for this evening. It was more that I could ever hope it would be," he whispered to her.

Seraphina did not have the chance to respond as the elevator doors opened to let them on, when on the other side of the doors was one Ryder Durand. She saw him before he saw her, and her loud sigh, brought the attention of both men.

"Well, well, what have we here," Ryder asked, zeroing in on Jason and how close he was standing next to Seraphina.

"Oh, for crying out loud, what are you doing here? Stalking me?" she asked, not moving from Jason's embrace.

"Ryder wasn't expecting to see you here. How do you know Seraphina?" Jason asked him, wondering what the story was.

"I was hoping to catch up with Seraphina, and she wasn't in her room, and now I see why," Ryder said, feeling very hurt and upset that she was with another man, especially the likes of one Jason Knecht. He knew Jason and knew he could break Seraphina.

"You didn't answer my question; why are you here?" she insisted, "I thought I had made myself quite clear."

"You did, but I was hoping to change your mind," Ryder said as the elevator door opened again.

"Good seeing you Ryder," Jason said as he gently guided her past the playboy and onto the elevator up to her suite. Once the doors were closed, he felt her relax, "Has he been bothering you?"

"No; he is my other client, and we have been working hard already, and he has shown me a few places and such. He's been great up to now, so seeing him was unexpected," she told him quietly.

"Ah, yea, I have heard he loves the chase; if you have to, change hotels and he will get the message," Jason suggested as he waited for her to open the door to her suite.

"I'm sure I won't need to. I have told him my rules, and he knows how I work, so, I hope he will behave himself," she said with a sigh.

"It'll be fine Seraphina, Ryder will eventually tire of the chase and find something easy to catch," Jason told her, helping her out of her coat and placing it on a chair.

"True. I knew about his reputation before I even met with him, but he still tries," she said as she turned to face Jason.

Jason did not say anything, instead, he gathered her up into his arms, "I hope you had a good time this evening before the whole Ryder thing," he said softly.

"I did, thank you. I had a lovely time with you," she replied, feeling secure in his arms, and not wanting the moment to end.

Instead, they both stood there for a few minutes, before Jason placed his hand under her chin, and brought her face up to his so he could gently kiss her.

She was not shocked, and knew he was silently asking for a kiss before their lips met. For her, time stood still as she lost herself in his kisses.

Jason eventually broke his kisses, needing air but still holding her tightly, feeling her heart beating against his own, "I feel so much for you, I know I promised I would not put you in the position to choose, and I will honor that," he said into her hair.

"Thank you; I appreciate you understanding my rules," she replied, feeling safe in his arms.

"Seraphina, please, give me tonight my love. Let me love you as you truly deserve," he whispered, desperately praying for her to say 'yes' to his request.

She was slightly shocked by his request, while her heart and body instantly agreed making her feel giddy, her brain was doing that 'what are you doing?' thing that it always did when she was close to breaking her rules for living. "Oh Jason," she started, not knowing exactly what to say. "God, I don't know," she started again, this time feeling tears at the corners of her eyes.

Jason cupped her face to look at his, saw the war within, and the tears beginning to form. "You do want this, but you're terrified, aren't you?" he asked quietly.

She did not say anything, instead nodded her head in agreement.

"Lovemaking is beautiful between two people who have deep feelings for one another, and it's so much more than just the physical act itself," he told her, hoping to ease whatever fears were there in her head. "I promise love not to hurt you."

And with that declaration, she took his hand, and led him to her bedroom. She was shaking with some unknown fear, and yet she was excited to feel that connection with someone she had been denied for so long.

Chapter 15

Jason gently turned her, so she was facing him, and he brought her close and started kissing her again. He was ecstatic that she had agreed, and a little apprehensive as he did not know where her fear was coming from.

He started slowly with his movements, caressing her face, arms and back before moving her closer to the bed. When her legs hit the edge of the bed, he stopped kissing her and gently placed her on the bed, mindful of her back and hip issues. He sat next to her looking deeply into her eyes as he allowed his hands to trail along her body, starting at her shoulder and slowly moving down to her toes before sliding his hand up the other side. He purposely avoided her erogenous zones, wanting her to trust his touches.

He continued to be slow with his movements as he brought his mouth to her neck to gently nibble causing her to moan in pleasure. That was music to his ears, and he continued to gently nip at her neck, moving from one side to the other. After a couple of minutes, he felt her hands on the buttons of his shirt, working to take the garment off him, which caused him to moan.

"Let me help you love," he whispered as he guided her hands on his shirt, helping her take it off his body. Once off, her hands explored his chest as did her eyes, taking in the muscles and hair. He let her explore, closely watching her face, until he felt her hand move lower towards his belt, "Patience my love, we have all night," he whispered as he laid her down again on the bed, kissing her as he started his slow work on her blouse, finding the ties behind her neck.

She helped him to lose her blouse, pulling it over her head and tossing it towards a chair in the corner before she returned her hands to his chest, "You're gorgeous," she murmured.

"And I think you are incredibly beautiful," he replied as he lay next to her, reveling in the feel of her soft skin. He gently slid his hand along her belly, feeling her taut muscles beneath her soft skin as his mouth started a trail from her neck to the edge of her bra.

"Please," she quietly begged, letting her body take the lead.

"Shh, love, we will get there, I promise," he whispered against her lips, before he moved to take off his pants and help her out of the skirt she was wearing. "You are amazing," he said as he looked at her legs; beautiful and shapely. He noted that she had scars on her sides, and below her hips, but he did not say anything, beginning to realize she had a traumatic event, and figured men would back out as soon as they saw her scars.

She knew he had seen some of her scars; and she had held her breath as he helped her with her skirt. She had always been self-conscious of those scars, and finally admitted to herself that they were her shield of protection from men hurting her. "You are still gorgeous," she said, laying back on the bed, taking in his powerful legs, and tented boxer-briefs.

He rejoined her on the bed, returning to kissing her body; worshipping her as she deserved. He wanted her to feel how much he already felt for her as he focused on her. He was also driving himself to distraction with his growing need for her. His body was demanding to hurry things along; but he also wanted to take the time to burn to his memory every single piece of her. He knew he would not have another chance with her.

He took his time with her, making sure that whatever skin he exposed got his full attention. When he unhooked and tossed her bra aside, he made sure to worship her incredible breasts, while hearing her gentle noises of pleasure.

Soon though, he couldn't take any more and his hands slid to her panties to gently slide them down her legs, giving him full access to her body. He moved to the end of the bed, and started at her feet once again, massaging and kissing his way up her body. When he reached the apex of her thighs, he stopped for a moment to caress her belly, watching her erratic breathing just before she grabbed his hand and holding it tightly, needing an anchor.

Jason noted that there were more scars, and he leaned over to kiss them gently, giving them the attention he thought she needed to accept herself. While he kissed those scars, his free hand went to her thighs and caressed them open to grant him entrance to the most sacred place of a woman. There, he moved so that he was between her open thighs and moved his mouth over her delicate folds, taking in her scent, wetness, and her complete beauty. He gently drew into his mouth her folds, playing with them with his tongue and lips hearing her sounds as he did so. "God, you are beautiful," he said, against her folds. "I never want to leave you, love."

"Jason, oh please," she begged him. She had reached her breaking point and was literally on the edge of an orgasm.

"A little more play my love," he said, feeling how taut her body was becoming and went back to what he was doing for her, knowing she was close to her release.

Her hand gripped his hand even tighter, while her other hand found his shoulder and had grabbed on for dear life. The harder he worked, the louder she got, and the harder he became. "Oh love, come for me, please," he asked her as his free hand moved to slide a finger into her molten core, feeling intense heat as he moved to watch her as she orgasmed.

He watched her as she gasped for breath, and her chest instantly became flushed as her blood moved quickly through her body. He continued to slide his finger in and out of her while his thumb gently stroked her clit as she exploded in a pleasure she had never experienced.

He patiently waited for her to float back to the bed, enjoying watching her breathing heavy, with her eyes closed, still firmly gripping his hand.

When she finally opened her eyes, she saw Jason sitting next to her, watching her intently, "How do you feel?" he asked her.

"Oh my god, I've never...," she trailed off, not too sure how to tell him that it was a hell of an orgasm he had given her.

"Shh, there's more for you my love," he told her as he stood to grab his pants, pulling out a couple of condoms and to shed his underwear.

"I want to please you too," she said, sitting up.

"You already have my love. You opened yourself to me and let me into a place no one else has been. I am truly honored that you chose me," he told her as he lay back on the bed next to her.

"Oh Jason," she started, not knowing what else to say.

He did not say anything, instead, he took her hand and placed it on his hardened cock, letting her explore and feel him.

He watched her as she stroked him before she sat up and moved to put him into her mouth. "Please love, you don't have to do that, I want tonight to be all about you," he said trying to stop her.

"I want to taste you," she said simply as she engulfed him with her mouth making him moan.

She felt him pulse in her mouth as she moved her tongue along his ridges and veins. Every so often, she would play with his tip, swiping up his pre-cum that was collecting there. "Please love stop, I want to be with you," he said as he gently eased her from his cock. He was so close to his release that he needed a few minutes to calm down before he became one with her.

He helped her to lay down before taking one of the condoms and opening the package so he could place the sheath on before moving over her.

There he kissed her, making sure her fire was ignited once again, wanting her to find pleasure at their joining. He felt her hands roam his body while he steadied himself above her, waiting for a signal from her that she was ready.

"Jason, please," she begged softly against his lips, needing to feel him inside her.

Jason was breathing heavy as he moved lower and placed his tip at her heated entrance. He looked at her face and saw a glow of sweat mixed with pleasure and need. He kissed her, then watched her closely as he slowly slid into her, feeling her burning heat throb around his cock. "God, you feel so right," he whispered, feeling a vice grip him as he slid out before sliding a little further in.

He heard and watched her gasp as he slid home, deeply encased within her, "Seraphina, are you alright?" He asked, wanting to make sure he had not hurt her in any way.

She nodded indicating she was alright and moved so that she was as close as she could be to him, melding her body with his, "Oh god," she said, looking into his eyes.

Jason started to move within her, never taking his eyes off her beautiful face as she too locked eyes with him. Together they moved as one, bringing each the pleasure they sought, slowly reaching for that pinnacle.

"Please, harder," she whispered to him as her body demanded more.

"Easy love, we will get there, I promise. Enjoy the sensations," he whispered back to her, wanting to please her on a whole new level.

As they continued their movements, he reveled in the noises she was making as her body grew hotter, very intense, and grip him even tighter than ever. "That's it love, let it build," he whispered, just before watching her come apart below him in ecstasy.

Feeling her intense orgasm brought him to the literal edge, and he needed a moment to stop and let her come down from her peak. He wanted her to experience one more before he allowed himself that pleasure of release. After a few moments, he resumed his movements, this time, he was a little quicker and harder, wanting her to feel the power that lovemaking could create.

Seraphina's sensations felt so new, yet she somehow remembered these sensations, and wanted more as Jason was bringing her to new heights. Just as she was floating back to the bed, he resumed his movements; they were quicker and harder keeping her at a level of arousal and need. Her lovemaking noises were louder as she wrapped her body tightly against his, needing as much contact with him as she could manage.

Once again, she reached that point where she was thrown into a time and space that did not exist on earth, and felt Jason come with her this time, hearing him as he let his body go with hers. Time stood still, and when they became conscious of their surroundings, Jason was breathing heavy as he laid on her. She felt him still within her, throbbing as his heart was beating erratically.

He moved his head and captured her lips in a heated yet loving kiss that seemed to last forever. "You are perfect," he said against her lips, before kissing her again.

Chapter 16

Seraphina woke very early from a short sleep. Today was the beginning of a new kind of hell; one she really was not looking forward to. She was tightly entwined in Jason's arms, feeling his even breath as he slept. While she lay there, she thought back to her decision to have Jason in her bed and the potential implication that it could cause. He promised that he would not interfere while she worked with Brandon Motorsports, but she also wondered if she would be able to focus having Jason close by, yet not able to connect with him. She also wondered if she was crazy to allow a man into her world after knowing him a very short time.

While she was deep in thought, Jason woke feeling Seraphina in his arms, not wanting to let her go. He knew he was gambling with his heart, and he really hoped that he would survive the next few months. He started to gently caress her belly feeling the softness of her skin. "Good morning," she said, softly feeling his hand.

"Good morning love, how did you sleep?" he asked.

"Uh, not too bad I think; really short though," she replied, turning to face him.

He snickered at her response, "Sorry love, I just can't help myself," he replied, before moving in for a kiss.

As their kisses grew more heated, Jason moved so that she could straddle him. He wanted her to take the lead if she wanted it again.

She felt the desire flare within her as she moved over him, still kissing. She sat and could feel him become hard with need, and she too felt a deep desire immediately flare within causing her to move back and forth upon him until he slid home.

She straightened up breaking the kiss, gasping with the feel of him deep within, throwing her head back. He watched her as she moved while his hands went to erect nipples, pinching and squeezing them as she started to ride him.

She controlled how fast and deeply he moved within her as her body heated with passion and need. Her fingers entwined in his chest hair, needing an anchor in the storm of need she was creating. "Oh yes," she chanted as she moved faster and harder upon him.

He moved his hands from her breasts to her hips, helping her move upon him, wanting her to find what she was seeking. Watching her face intently and seeing all the need, a little frustration, and pleasure play upon her face. "That's it love, do what you need," he encouraged as he moved one hand from her hip to where their bodies joined, finding that little erect nub and started to gently rub it.

She felt his hand rubbing as fast as she was thrusting, and it was all she needed to find that exquisite release her body craved. It was so intense that her body spasmed while letting go of a flood of pleasure throughout her entire body and from her most intimate place.

Jason felt her intense orgasm and felt the whoosh from her body, watching her twitch above, bringing his own intense orgasm, flooding her with his seed.

It took several minutes for them to float back to earth. Seraphina was sprawled over Jason, feeling quite boneless, still breathing heavy. Jason too was still breathing heavily as his hands kept a firm grip on her. It took a few minutes for him to realize he was still inside of her, never wanting to leave.

"This, I think is going to be much harder than I thought," he murmured into her neck.

She sighed, knowing exactly what he was talking about, "Fuck, maybe we should've waited until everything's been completed," she said, playing with some chest hair with her fingers.

"I don't know if that would've made a difference," he said moving to look at her.

"I think it would have; keeping my distance from anything emotional is what got me to where I am today," she told him as she sat up on him. "This..," she said as she softly waved her hand between them, "has never been part of my life, and I don't know why I let you into my very private life. I don't regret it; this has been the most amazing experience, but I know my judgment might be colored differently now, and I'm not too sure what that will look like, or even how to handle that," she told him softly.

Jason was quiet for a moment, taking in what she told him. She kept everything and everyone at an arms distance to ensure she could work without emotion. "I get it; you prefer to work with no emotion. Humans are emotional creatures, and we need our emotions to guide us love; don't be scared by what you feel now, it could help you too," he said gently, hoping she could see the positive in this very new change for her. "You help companies with change; keeping them on the leading edge," he started, and she nodded in agreement, "but, you don't like change, and really who does?" he asked, causing her to snicker.

"God, I know, I think you just figured me out to a T," she said with mirth.

"I want you to see this as a positive; I know for me it is, and it's something I am keeping close to my heart until you and I can resume this," he told her seriously.

She thought for a moment, "Well, I think you are right, this is positive; I just have to learn how to keep it that way," she said as he leaned in for a kiss. "And now, I have to get moving before Grant pounds on my door wondering where I am.

"Who's Grant?" he asked as she got off him hoping to hear that the other man she mentioned was not another lover.

"He is my counterpart, my right-hand and best friend; he runs this company with me and prefers to be in the background, while I am the face of the company. He and I go way back, and his wife Kelley is also my best friend," she told him as she quickly checked her phone, before moving towards the bathroom.

"Ah, I see, and he will want to start early, eh?" he asked, following her into the bathroom.

"God, yea, he is an early bird that one. Still drives me crazy that he gets up at like five and thinks everyone else should be up too. I am not an early bird, and some mornings are a struggle for me," she said as he turned on the shower.

The couple finished breakfast before Jason had to admit to himself that it was time; he needed to leave her to do her job. "I really don't want to do this, but I know I have to," he said to her when they were at the door, saying good-bye.

"I know, I have loved having you here with me, and now hope I can get this finished quickly," she stated before he moved in for a loving kiss.

"If you do need me, please love, I'm only a call away," he told her, when he broke the kiss.

He did not get the chance to say anything more as there was a quick and efficient knock at her door. He was slightly startled by the knock but saw that she was not and had rolled her eyes, giving him another quick kiss before opening the door.

"Grant, what a lovely surprise," she said as both Grant and Jason came face to face with Seraphina standing off to the side.

"Morning boss, are you ready to get this shit show going?" Grant asked as he started to move past the couple. "Hi, I'm Grant, I sure hope she mentioned me to you," he said to Jason.

"Jason, and yes, she did. Good luck on the projects. Seraphina," he added much more quietly, "thank you love, know you are in my heart." He told her before he walked out of her suite, towards the elevators.

She watched him, "Good-bye Jason," she said before the elevator doors opened and she retreated into her suite where Grant was waiting.

Once the door was shut, she turned to see Grant standing near the windows looking out, however, his reflection showed a shit-eating grin on his face, "Grant, I swear, I will kill you if you don't get that grin off your face," she said, quite sternly.

"Hey, I'm really happy for you," he said, turning to face her. "You needed this, and I think it's great that you found someone," he said.

"Yea, well, it was a one-time thing," she said to him, pulling out the four binders she had going for the clients. "Nothing more can happen between us," she confirmed to him. "Now, can we concentrate on what is guaranteed to be a living hell for the next three or so months?" she asked, already feeling a headache come on.

Chapter 17

The weeks flew by in a flurry of intense activity. Seraphina had her entire focus on both projects, trying to get the impossible accomplished in a speed they have never worked at before.

One thing that was a bit of a thorn in her side was Ryder. As a client, he was great to work with and all her consultants and contractors loved his sense of humor. She had to admit, he was fun some days. But, there were days when he would insist on dinner with her, seeming to try and bend her rules for him. He was very charming, and she noted that his focus was solely on her. He had not looked at another woman as her team had told her on more than one occasion. There were days when Ryder was the cause of her headaches, wanting things his way. She also had to laugh because there were some very tense moments, and he was the one to break the tension with one of his well-timed one-liners. She had to admit, Ryder definitely kept her attention, and she found that she looked forward to spending time with him.

Ryder wanted to keep a close watch on Seraphina, making sure Jason had not hurt her in any way. He was scared that she would continue to keep him at arm's length, while he wanted to be as close as he dared to her.

Jason on the other hand, kept his promise to her and had left her to work. When he saw her on campus, he took great pains to avoid her, not wanting to cause her undue stress she figured. He had not contacted her in any form, and he made sure that he was not at any meeting that she would be attending. Instead, he would send one of his counterparts to the meeting with some excuse as to why he could not go. Some of his co-workers were beginning to wonder what was going on with him as he would be in the center of any change in the company, and yet, with all the major changes that were being made, he was nowhere to be found.

Seraphina too wondered about him and if the words he had said to her were true or a ploy to get her into bed with him. The more she tried to run into him, the harder he worked to avoid her. She was past frustrated with him and had sent him an email requesting a meeting. He never responded to her email. That made her even grumpier, she thought they did have a connection, and when she realized her mistake, of course it was too late to wipe the memory of him. "Fuck, I knew it; even though I wanted it as a one-time thing, I thought we had a connection, dammit," she mumbled to herself one day when she saw Jason at the end of a hall, he had not seen her, but as soon as he did, he immediately turned around and fled from her.

Grant figured out quite quickly that Seraphina had two men after her; one managed his way into her bed while the other was being open about his interest in her. He wondered about Jason and Ryder; and why Seraphina was so hell-bent on this project. She was working herself into the ground with the impossibly long hours she was keeping. He knew these projects could either make or break them, and while the company was surpassing expectations and timeline, she was beginning to suffer. He could see dark circles under her eyes, and he noted that she was not eating properly. "Dammit, Kelley's going to kill me if I let Seraphina continue like this," he muttered to himself, rubbing his face as another meeting wrapped up with Ryder and his team.

Ryder also noticed that Seraphina was working herself into the ground on these projects. "Ok Seraphina," he said, after the meeting, with Grant listening in, "you need to go back to your hotel, have a bath, some dinner and sleep. This stuff is not going anywhere, and I'm positive that all this will still be here tomorrow morning," he told her with a very concerned look on his face.

"Ryder, I'm fine, I normally look like this halfway through a project," she said with some humor. "We are over the halfway mark with you, thank god."

"I'm well aware of how hard you're working, and I know there's another client that you've been concentrating on as well. Mr. Brandon let it slip that you're working on his company at an owner's meeting we had last week," he said.

"Oh, that man, I swear he'd forget his head if it weren't attached," she grumbled, "so much for confidentiality, eh?"

"You knew it was only a matter of time before everyone knew we were playing with two competitors. And, for the record Ryder, you and Mr. Brandon want completely different things from us, and why we agreed to the both of you at the same time," Grant piped in before Seraphina lost it. He could see her brewing under the surface.

"Yea, I know that; he told us that you guys were working miracles for his company. He's been singing your praises to others," Ryder told them.

"Well, if anything, maybe this will generate more business Seraphina," Grant said.

She sighed as she closed her eyes for a moment and rubbed her head. "Fuck my head hurts," she mumbled. "Alright, back to what we have left to do," she said, trying to get the focus back on work.

"Nope, I am taking you to your hotel so you can rest," Ryder insisted.

"I agree Sera, Kelley would kill me if she saw you right now; go rest," Grant told her, trying to shoo her out the door.

"Jesus," she swore, "Give me the strength not to kill someone!"

Grant laughed, "Hey, if you can catch me, you can try," he told her.

"Oh, go take a flying leap into hell," she snarked at him, with a big grin.

"Ah sweetheart, I'm already there!" Grant laughed as he left.

"Seraphina, you are not going to win this battle, please, let me take you back to your hotel so you can eat and rest," Ryder told her gently once they were alone. He walked to where she was, and took her into his arms, "I am worried that you're going to burn out very soon."

"I'll be fine Ryder, really. This is pretty much normal for me," she told him softly.

"Please indulge me this time," Ryder softly insisted.

She looked at the concerned look he had on his face, and sighed, "Fine," she replied as she broke from his embrace to finish packing up her briefcase.

Together they quietly left the campus with Ryder guiding her to his vehicle and helping her get in. Once they were on the road Ryder asked, "How are things with Mr. B?"

"They are going alright; his needs are very different from yours and as we've progressed these last several weeks, we found more areas that needed immediate attention than what we were originally hired for," she said. "That's about all I can tell you."

"I'm not looking for specifics; I'm trying to figure out why you look so run down," he told her gently, taking her hand into his.

She laughed softly, "I'm serious here, and I do normally look quite haggard at the halfway mark as most things at this stage are resting with me. Once we move forward towards resolutions and such, the pressure will begin to come off me and then I start to look normal again. Its stress with me that make me short-tempered, caffeine addicted, and very tired looking," she told him, looking at him.

"I'm making sure that you don't add any undue stress," he told her. "You're already doing so much for me and I'm sure Mr. B; I think you need a couple of assistants to help you."

"Ah, I tried that route; most can't keep up with the way I think and do things. Only Grant has been closest to the mark, and even then, he has assistants to help him keep up with everything on his plate," she told him. "I know I work too hard, it's a flaw, and I admit it's there. It's also why I'm successful too. Work is my life, and why at forty, I'm single, no kids, no previous relationships for god, many, many years, only my job. Don't get me wrong, I love my job and what I have accomplished; I have done so much for myself and others. I do have hobbies that help me manage, but I will always be all about work."

"Holy shit; you're serious? You have ignored life for work? That's crazy! I get the whole workaholic thing, as sometimes my focus is like that; but there comes a point when you have to live. Look at it this way; when you pass away, who's going to mourn and miss you? What will be said in your eulogy? You have to leave some legacy behind, but it can't just be about work!" he exclaimed as they pulled into the valet service at the hotel.

Seraphina did not say anything, instead, she thought about the words Ryder said, and mulled them over as they walked together, towards the bank of elevators.

Ryder guided her towards her suite, not saying anything as he knew she was thinking about what he had said. Once they were in her room, he put her things on the chair that was designated for her briefcase, before sitting on the sofa, waiting for her to come out of her thought process.

She looked at Ryder, "I'm not too sure how I can answer your questions. You are right, I have completely ignored the fact that life has passed me by. I've likely reached the halfway point in my life, and I have nothing to show for it except my company, and how that's grown into something amazing. But, except for Grant, Kelley, Kayla, and my staff, no one would miss or mourn me," she said as she sat next to Ryder, feeling quite defeated.

"Seraphina, it's never too late to begin living; you have to learn how to balance life with work," he told her gently as he cupped her face and brought his to hers capturing her lips in a kiss. "I can help you Seraphina, if you'll let me."

"Ryder, seriously, you know I can't," she told him when they broke the kiss. "I need to keep my life compartmentalized. It's how I manage everything, especially me."

"I'm simply telling you that I can give you everything you've ever desired. Please babe, you know that we are good together!" he exclaimed.

"I know that," she muttered as she rubbed her face, "Ryder, please, can you just leave this alone for now? I can't deal with all this at the moment," she quietly pleaded.

Chapter 18

$\mathcal{S}$eraphina and her company had reached the end of the three-month mark on the two projects; one was very nearly completed, on schedule and within budget too. She was just working on the finishing touches; recommendations that she would pass onto Ryder as her company's final parting gift to him. The three binders she was working on were divided into specific sections, starting with the ones of most importance to least. Her team had worked very hard to get this project done on time. She was still exhausted, and she was really feeling it, but she powered through her exhaustion, wanting these two projects to be done.

The other project however, hit a standstill, and she was pretty sure they would not move past it to complete the project. It had to do with the succession plan, and Seraphina knew this could be very sticky. When she went over the itemized contract that Mr. Brandon had signed, she made it very clear that she and her company would create a solid succession plan, and find suitable candidates based upon the needs of the company, not personal feelings, or a need to keep everything 'in-house" as she found Mr. Brandon preferred to do. The big issue was, while they were looking outside the organization to find executives for Brandon Motorsports, Mr. B had gone behind Seraphina's back and promised the VP and CFO positions to employees of his that he thought should continue the business. They were already inside the organization and held roles that were important to the company. So, while Seraphina found some very highly sought-after executives to come work for Brandon Motorsports, Mr. Brandon promoted from within and had prevented Seraphina from learning about it until he saw fit.

When she found out what Mr. Brandon had done, she blew a gasket. She was very blunt with her words to him and his current team of newly hired executives regarding the waste of her and her very highly skilled team's time. One person that Seraphina had never considered and been blindsided by, and was promoted to the VP position, was Jason. That made her blood boil something fierce. She brought out the contract Mr. Brandon signed, stood next to him, and started making large circles around the date, his signature beside each agreed upon item her company had been hired to do, before she went over to the last page, again, showing him and his new team of the penalty that was also in the contract for wasting their time. When she was finished, she did not give Mr. Brandon a chance to refute her statements, instead, she walked out, leaving Grant to deal with that mess.

"God fucking dammit," she spewed as she walked down the hall. She had seen many heads poking out from their offices and knew the building had heard her tirade. "I should have known that bastard was playing me. He probably fucking knew what was going to happen."

She stopped just outside the building entrance, and took a very long, deep, and slow breath to try and calm herself. She was shaking with anger, and that was causing her not to feel too good. "God, now what," she muttered when she heard her name. She turned, and saw Jason running after her.

"Seraphina, please, let me explain," he started.

She, however, was not interested in anything he had to say to her, "Please just fuck off." She told him, before turning her back to him, and started walking toward her vehicle.

"Please love, please," he begged her.

"You don't get to call me that," she demanded, as she turned to face him, her anger clear on her face. "You fucked me over, and I let you into a place that no one has been in a very long time. I gave you my body, and you knew this whole fucking time what was going to happen!" she exclaimed, pointing a finger at his chest.

"Seraphina, I'm sorry, really!" he tried, but she was not having any of it.

"Just admit to me that this was all a fucking game!" she said, this time waiting for a response, crossing her arms across her chest.

Jason looked at her, saw how tired and stressed she looked, and he saw the intense anger flaring in her eyes. He was not too sure what to say that would calm her down. He sighed, "I am sorry; I never thought I would feel a connection with you the way I did. I was supposed to take you to dinner and distract you from the project. I still have feelings for you Seraphina," he told her softly.

"You bastard," she said feeling tears welling up in her eyes, "I let you in, god dammit, and this was just a game to you. Men like you are the reason I don't have relationships! I do not ever want to see your face again, and if I find out you've been telling people that you managed to bed me, I will have your balls on a silver platter, you got that? I have special skill sets that you know nothing about," she told him very quietly.

Jason felt his blood run cold as she talked to him, and he knew she meant every word as her anger towards him was very clear. "I am sorry," he told her once more, before she turned on her heel, and walked the short distance to her car.

He watched her get in and drive the car out of the parking lot. He was so absorbed watching her that he had not heard Grant come up behind him.

"If I were you, I'd run," Grant told him. "She is so past the being pissed mark, that she really will rip your balls off, trust me, she could do it if she's mad enough," he said, before making his way to his own car. "And I'd never breathe a word about bedding her either; she can make your life a living hell, she has some amazing contacts in very high places."

Seraphina drove straight to her hotel wanting desperately to work off some of the anger that was coursing through her body. Once she was in the safety of her room, she dissolved into tears. She let her guard down, just once and it bit her in the ass. She thought she had made a good decision this time. That thought alone made her feel sick, making her sit for a bit to try and settle her stomach. "Damn nerves," she muttered. She eventually walked into the bathroom, where she scrubbed her face clean, and started a bath for herself. She was grabbing herself some water to take with her when there was a knock on the door.

She answered it to find Grant, "Hey, how goes the hairy mess?" she asked as she let him into her room, finally feeling a little more in control of her varying emotions.

"Oh, it's a mess alright; Mr. Brandon honestly thought he was within his rights to promote from within, even though I know you went through the contract line by line. So, I told him we would be stopping the project, we will be submitting the final bill, with the penalty that covers all the costs associated with us having to break our own contracts and such, and if he doesn't pay, we have no issues taking this one to court."

"Hang on," she replied, going to shut off the running water for her bath. She returned a minute later, "Good; the sooner we all can head home the better. I'm done with North Carolina and all this racing shit," she said, sitting down.

"You're looking quite pale, you ok?" Grant asked, concerned.

"Yea, just my nerves got to me as I had to face the man who had me," she stated flatly. "I thought I knew better this time."

"Hey, he played you; even I didn't pick up on it until we were told he was to be VP," Grant told her.

"God I am so embarrassed; I let a man in. The first man in years that I willingly let touch me. I don't know if I can ever trust a man now," she said, looking at Grant.

He sighed, and took her hand into his, "I'm so sorry Sera, not all of us men are like that, and you know this. I just might take a crack at that bastard for you. He broke your heart," he said.

"I'm not sure if it was my heart, or something else; I do know that I'm done with trying to understand, and I'm done wishing for love, and a family," she responded, getting up, and walking into the bathroom, shutting the door behind her.

Later that evening, she had just wrapped up a couple of loose ends for Ryder; they would be officially done his project tomorrow. She had to admit, they did the job in the timeframe given; something she did not think was remotely possible. She snickered at her thoughts, "God that was a hell of a ride," she said to herself, as she placed the table of contents into the binders.

Once she was finished, she leaned back on the sofa and closed her eyes. Her head was still pounding, and she still was not feeling too good either. 'Well, when was the last time you ate dummy?' She thought to herself. "I ate lunch, thank you very much," she said out loud, bringing her own fight to herself out. "Well, if it isn't food, then what is it?"

"Hell, if I know! It is flu season, so any kind of bug is highly possible. Get some sleep, you'll feel better tomorrow," she told herself with a laugh. "See, I can officially tell Grant that I have gone insane; I've had a complete conversation with myself," she said, getting up from where she was sitting, still laughing at herself. Shaking her head, she turned off the lights and went to her bedroom where she had a drink of water, took some medication for her headache before crawling into bed. She made sure her alarm was set, then turned off the light and let sleep overtake her.

Chapter 19

Seraphina was spending her last night in North Carolina going to dinner with Ryder. He wanted to do something special for her. He watched how hard she worked on the project for him and his company, and he loved the extra her company provided; a laundry list of things they identified as required changes that would need to be implemented in the coming months and years. That, he was not expecting, and was touched that they went that extra to ensure his company remained successful for years to come. He had not asked for any of that, and Seraphina had told him that it was a parting gift to their client. All their clients would get a list and whether they followed that list was no longer their problem. However, it was easy to figure out which clients followed their recommendations.

On this evening, Ryder picked her up from her hotel room looking dasher in pressed slacks, collared shirt, and sport jacket. When Seraphina opened the door to reveal a neat and tidy Ryder, she was a little surprised. "Why, Ryder, you do own more than just t-shirts and jeans," she remarked to him, with mirth in her voice.

"Ah, yea, I do. Sometimes I must schmooze with potential partners and sponsors, hence the non-jeans look," he told her ,with a big grin.

She thought about that for a moment, "I recall someone saying that sometimes a suit was needed for those kinds of meetings."

"It depends on who you are schmoozing with, most are more business casual these days, and formal suits are left to those legal people," he said as he helped her with her coat.

"Ah, gotcha," she replied, "so, where are we going for dinner?" she asked.

"I thought we would try this new steakhouse that just opened up. Kind of high end with amazing food," he told her as they waited for the elevator.

"That sounds lovely," she replied, thinking a steak sounded very good to her.

The drive was a comfortable quiet as they had gotten used to each other and did not feel the need to fill the quiet with mindless talk. The radio was on low playing some easy jazz. "You know, for late winter, it seems to be a beautiful night out," she said, taking in the warm weather with the gentle breeze.

"It is unseasonably warm tonight," he agreed, "I heard shit really hit the fan with your other client," Ryder stated.

"You, and I think the entire racing world heard me. Damn man; he hires us to make him a succession plan, and then decides to hire from within, regardless of their capacity to actually run the company or not. I was very pissed, and I know the whole building heard me," she said, getting fired up again at the memory. "So, I stopped work, and will send him my bill with the penalty that he signed in the contract, plus any additional fees we incurred by breaking our contracts early with our vendors and contractors."

"Makes sense; when I heard what happened, I was so happy that I didn't break any contract agreements," he said with a snicker. "I never want to be on the receiving end of your anger."

"Ah, you have been quite lucky I admit; most clients are not as lucky. When we start implementing the changes phase, that is when they start being stupid and I have to yell and remind them of why they hired me. If they are going to spend millions on me, they should at least hear what I have to say and see what I can do for them," she told him.

"I am happy that I hired you; we are in great shape and will be for a long time to come," he agreed.

"I'm glad that you are happy with the job we did; I pour a part of my soul into every project, and I have to admit, your project was a lot of fun. I'm not too sure if we found you that unicorn, but we tried very hard," she told him softly as he pulled up to the restaurant. "This place looks very cool with its smooth and modern look."

"Food is supposed to be amazing too," he told her as he helped her out of the car. "It's not a good back and hip day today, eh?"

"It's not as bad as other days, just needing a little extra to make sure I don't stoop and cause more issues," she told him as they walked into the building.

They were seated in a beautiful corner where they had some privacy but were not hidden away. As they were looking at the menu, Ryder selected a bottle of wine for them to share before they ordered.

"This place is very nice; I like the ambiance; soft music and the background noise seems muted so it's not as loud as other places," she noted, "it's very comfortable."

"I'm glad you like this place. I wanted this last night to be a good one for you. I am also quite sad that you will be leaving tomorrow. I have loved having you nearby, working with me, and being my friend," Ryder told her, taking her hand into his. "I am still hoping that you and I can move towards more than friendship. You've gotten to know me, and I have you, I think we could be good together."

"Oh Ryder, you are a sweet man. Yes, I have gotten to know you quite well. But you also know how I work; that means literally no time for a relationship or really to live. I know we have talked about this at great length, and I don't know if I can trust or change," she told him, squeezing his hand. "I thought I had made a good decision, but now I don't think I can trust myself, let alone anyone else."

He looked deep into her eyes, and saw that war she always had, "Sera, I don't know what happened to you to cause you to not trust men and shy away from relationships, and I'm not even going to pretend to even try to know. Something happened to you; maybe someone broke your heart into a million pieces, maybe you had something traumatic happen, I don't know. You, beautiful Seraphina, are deserving of love and all the wonderful things that come with it; security, intimacy, love, friendship, a confidante, a lover, and so much more. You deserve that," he told her gently, while stroking her cheek. "I have feelings for you, and I have respected your boundaries even though it was so hard to do."

Seraphina had no words for him, and felt tears spring to her eyes as his words pierced her in a place she had kept locked away. She wiped her eyes, embarrassed that she was showing so much emotion.

"I'm sorry Sera, I really am. I didn't mean to hurt you in any way," he said softly as he wiped away a stray tear. "Please don't let what I said continue to hurt you, alright? I just want this evening to be enjoyable before you have to leave."

"I'm sorry Ryder, I didn't mean to kill the mood or evening. I don't know why I'm so emotional lately, but I know you were trying to be the friend who tells me what I need to hear," she said. "I love that about you; you make me laugh, and you've shown me not to take some things as seriously as I used to. You are an amazing man; it's me who has the issues and I know this, and I don't want you to feel you have to wait for me to sort out my head."

"Shh, Sera, no matter what happens, lets agree to remain friends, even if we don't move forward," he told her.

"Thank you, I would like that very much," she told him as their dinner arrived.

Once they finished dinner, and the bottle of wine consumed, "Sera, how about you and I take a drive, I'm not ready to let you go yet," he told her.

"That sounds nice, sure, maybe we can find a nice little place for a drink before the evening ends," she agreed, not wanting her time with him to end just yet. She greatly enjoyed dinner with his stories of the latest pranks the teams were playing on one another.

She had a chance to play a prank on the teams near the end of the project. She had sent one of her consultants to go to the team's meeting and tell them that the teams were going to be changed around. She had prepared a list of who would work with whom, knowing that all of them would freak out. Sure enough, all of them had come running to Ryder, who had known about what Seraphina had done, and told them it was all settled and to get on with learning how to work with each other. It took them all a half day before they returned to Ryder, literally on their knees, begging him to undo the changes. It was funny to see all these grown men stuffed into Ryder's office, on their knees begging. Seraphina took a video of them begging, and as she came up behind them, scared them with a quiet 'gotcha.'

"Please tell me that your drivers have decided to be a little more open to using technology to help them learn the tracks and equipment; that simulator was very expensive," she asked.

"Oh, believe me, they love that thing. I've had to put a sign-up sheet with time limits now," he confirmed as he led her to the car and helped her get in.

"That's good; the fighting was I think the biggest headache with the teams," she recalled.

"God, no kidding; that thing was expensive and for them to tell me they didn't need no computer to tell them how to drive was one headache I dreaded. Now they have all had the chance to work with it and they love it," he said as they drove.

"That will make them even more competitive than the other drivers which will make you a winning owner," she said as she watched the scenery pass her by.

"That will be fantastic," Ryder agreed.

Chapter 20

Ryder had taken them to a dark and remote area, and as he led her down a path, she wondered what he was up to. "Exactly where are we going?" she asked threading her way along the path following him while holding his hand.

"There is this really neat place where it's sheltered from wind and has an awesome view of the stars. They are so bright that it's amazing. Huge diamonds in the sky twinkling and winking at you," he told her as he helped her along the path.

When they arrived at the spot, it was sheltered by three large rocks, and had benches to sit on while you looked up at the universe. He found them a place to sit and then showed her what he knew. He fully admitted that astronomy was not his strong suit, but did admit that this was a great place to watch the stars and contemplate life.

"I get that; its quiet for the most part, quite warm, and those stars are so bright, you want to reach out and touch them. Makes you feel small and yet makes you wonder what else is out there," she said still looking up.

"Exactly," he agreed as he sat closely next to her and wrapped an arm around her. She shifted so that she could lean against him as she continued to look up.

"This is incredible, and quite the hidden little gem you've found," she said, after a few minutes.

"It's not so hidden; there are a lot of people that will be here all night, but it's also big enough to give space for all to enjoy on their own. I love coming here on nights I need to think without distractions. I get fresh air, and I just let my mind work through a problem or issue. Its great if I need to figure out a solution. Just letting my mind wander with the stars helps me to think clearly," he told her softly.

"I totally get that," she said, still looking up. "This place has a vibration that screams to me in a very good way; not sure why, but I love this place."

Together they sat looking up and enjoying the quiet of the evening. "Ryder," she started, after a while, "I think I might like to try to have a relationship with you. I can't continue to be scared about the 'what if', and I at some point have to learn to trust."

"I don't know what happened, and I'm glad you think that you and I are worth pursuing. Logistics might be a little issue, but if we're meant to be, then we can overcome anything," he said softly before he closed the gap between them and gently kissed her.

After several minutes Ryder suggested they head back to her hotel for a night cap, helping her up from the bench and walking with her to the car.

"Thank you for such a lovely evening," she said as he pulled onto the roadway.

"Thank you for agreeing to dinner, it's been a great night. You know, it doesn't have to end this early." he replied as he pulled out of the parking lot and drove towards the hotel.

"What are you suggesting Mr. Durand?" she asked with a small grin.

Ryder started laughing and looked at her before taking her hand and kissing it, "Well, it's kind of like this..." he started. Before he could continue his sentence, they heard a horn blast just before they were struck from the passenger side by another vehicle. Ryder had missed the stop sign and crossed into the path of an oncoming truck.

The car they were in spun around a couple of times at what looked like high velocity. Ryder was unaware of what happened and was knocked unconscious while the vehicle moved about, throwing the couple inside around violently. After what seemed like forever, there were people coming to help the couple in the car that was struck, including the person who hit them.

"Oh god, are you alright? I thought you were going to stop! God, I'm sorry, I didn't have time to stop either," the young man said in a rush, checking on Ryder, his hands shaking from shock.

An older woman came over to help, and helped the man, "Its ok, it was an accident, the police and ambulance are coming, let's see if you're ok too," she said as she took the driver of the truck over to the side of the road, while other people tended to Ryder and Seraphina.

Ryder regained consciousness after a couple of minutes, "Fuck, what happened?" he muttered quietly, moving his hand to his head. "My head is killing me."

"You must have hit your head on the steering wheel," a man told him. "Ambulance is on the way," he said as sirens grew louder by the second.

Ryder concentrated on his breathing, trying to ease the pain in his head. It took him a minute or so to remember Seraphina was in the passenger seat, "Oh God, Sera!" he exclaimed, trying to move his head to look at her.

"Hey, hey, please keep your head still, you might have a neck injury," the man helping him said.

"Seraphina, please check on her," Ryder begged, scared that something happened to her.

"She's ok; someone is caring for her, take it easy. Here are the experts to help you and your wife," the man said to him, stepping back to let the paramedics care for the injured couple.

As soon as the paramedics were in sight of Ryder, he lost consciousness once again.

Ryder woke sometime later in the hospital. He groaned and opened his eyes, seeing bright lights, closed them with another groan. "Fuck, what happened," he muttered.

"Hey, you're awake! This is great, I'm Dr. Jones, how do you feel?" the doctor asked as he walked into his room.

"I feel like crap; what happened?" Ryder asked.

"You don't remember? Ok; you were in a vehicle accident, and from the tests, you have minor injuries, cuts and such, and a concussion," Dr. Jones told him softly, going over to him. "Let me check your eyes," he said, taking his pen light and flashing them into his eyes. "Good, they're both responsive. You are going to have a very big headache for a while; there is quite the goose egg on your forehead from where you hit the steering wheel. The air bags didn't deploy for some reason."

"So, how long am I in here for," Ryder asked, closing his eyes against the light.

"Well, I'd like to keep you at least one more night just to be sure I haven't missed anything," he told him.

He leaned back, and closed his eyes, before they flew open and he sat up quickly, "What about Sera?" He asked in a panic, feeling his head throb from the movement. "Ouch!"

"Easy, easy, she's in surgery," the Dr. Jones said as he tried to soothe him. "She sustained serious injuries and needed surgery to repair a fairly large tear in her spleen and another small tear in her kidney. Last I checked, she and your baby were doing very well," the doc said softly, helping Ryder to lay back on the bed.

As Ryder lay back on the bed, "Oh thank god," he said feeling a little better, "Wait, baby?"

"Yes, your wife is about eighteen weeks pregnant," he confirmed.

"Holy fuck, she didn't tell me!" Ryder exclaimed, feeling numb wash over him in a wave from the news.

"She may have been waiting until the danger zone passed as she is older and miscarriage is a big possibility," he told Ryder, trying to calm him down. "Once she is finished surgery, she will be brought into your room so you're together. Oh, and a Grant Larson is also here for the both of you and is worried," Dr. Jones commented.

"Grant. Fuck, he is going to be pissed," Ryder muttered, rubbing his face.

"Ah, you do know him, great, I will send him in," Dr. Jones said as he left the room.

Ryder laid there, eyes closed, trying to digest the news that Seraphina was pregnant. "Why didn't she say anything to me about the baby?" He wondered.

Grant quietly walked in to see Ryder laying there, looking quite battered, "Hey, you ok?" he asked quietly.

"Umm, I have a concussion, and the obvious bumps and bruises and a couple of cuts. I didn't know Seraphina was pregnant; did you?" Ryder said, without preamble.

"What? Sera's pregnant?" Grant asked, shocked, his eyes going wide at the news.

"That's what the doc just told me. She sustained more serious injuries than I did and is now in surgery to repair tears in her spleen and kidney and she and baby were doing well. I had no idea. Did she tell you she was pregnant? And she finally agreed to a relationship with me and did not tell me she was pregnant," Ryder mused, sadly.

"Hey, listen to me; I didn't know she was pregnant. I'm sure the guy responsible was a one-night stand. I think I know who it was, and I am going to go beat the living crap out of him. I wonder if he did that on purpose to Sera," Grant said, feeling intense anger that Jason would do that to her.

"Grant, please tell me, who's the one-night stand?" Ryder begged quietly, wondering if she had told them of their night together.

Grant sighed, and thought for a moment, "Its Jason Knecht; he was very smooth in seducing her, and we found out later that he was tasked with distracting Seraphina so Brandon Motorsports could do their thing behind our backs, he knew he was going to be the VP before we were even hired."

"That fucker had and threw away Sera?" Ryder asked quietly, feeling his anger begin to rise to the surface.

"Yup, he did. She felt extremely used and embarrassed that she chose to let him have her, and well, there's some shit that happened way back that has caused her to not trust people, but that is her story to tell, I can't," Grant told him, trying to control his anger as the door opened.

Seraphina was brought into the room. Attached were various monitors and tubes. It took the hospital staff several minutes to get her settled into her bed and ensured that all the monitors and such were set properly to monitor her. There was one monitor that Ryder was very fascinated with, and that was the one monitoring the baby's heartbeat.

A Near Miss

Grant felt his anger dissipate as soon as he saw her; looking battered and bruised, instead he felt his heart break at seeing her like that.

Ryder felt tears spring to his eyes as he looked at her, so small and fragile in the bed next to him. One nurse noticed, and went over to Ryder, "She looks a lot worse than she really is; surgery was a success, and she and baby are doing very well, but let her rest, her body needs the time to heal," she said gently, rubbing his hand.

"God, she looks broken," Ryder warbled, feeling his tears spill onto his cheeks.

"I know she looks bad; the bruising will fade, as will the bumps and abrasions. Considering the car was hit from the passenger side, it's amazing that she wasn't more seriously hurt. She is doing great; I promise," the nurse said.

"God, Kelley is going to freak," Grant murmured. "Sera's pregnant, and didn't tell anyone," he said still looking at her. "I'm going to go make some calls, I'll be back in a little while. Is there anything you need Ryder?"

"Huh?" Ryder said, not paying attention and looked at Grant, who rolled his eyes. "No, I think I'm ok for now," he said, returning his attention to Seraphina.

Grant quietly left the room, leaving Ryder to his thoughts. First though, Grant had a few calls he had to make, the first would be to his wife, and Seraphina's best friend, then, he was going to make an appointment to meet with Jason so he could beat the living shit out of him for hurting Seraphina and then leaving her pregnant. "Bastard," he muttered as he started his phone calls.

Chapter 21

Grant was waiting impatiently for Jason to meet him. He made sure all was in place before he arranged to meet Jason at an out of the way, small coffee shop as he did not want anyone to know he was planning on castrating Jason. He finished his coffee when he saw a very expensive vehicle pull up to the shop and Jason get out. "Figures, the bastard did it for the money."

Jason walked in and saw Grant there waiting for him, "You mentioned you wanted to talk, and it was important," he said, getting down to business.

"That is very true, and I have some questions for you. First, what are your feelings and intentions towards Seraphina?" Grant asked bluntly as the waitress brought Jason over a cup of coffee and refilled Grant's cup, "Thank you."

Jason sat there for a moment before taking a swallow of his coffee, "I'm not too sure what you mean," he said.

"Ok, what are your feelings for Seraphina? This is important, alright?" Grant tried again.

"Well, I have feelings for her; but I can't move forward with anything now. Why, does she want a relationship?" Jason asked as he picked up his cup, but this time with his left hand.

It took Grant a moment for his brain to register a wedding ring on Jason's hand. "How long have you been married?" he asked, changing directions for a moment, his eyes narrowing in contempt.

"Umm, almost two years, why?" Jason asked.

"Holy fuck, you slept with Seraphina, and you're married? I am gob smacked here. Why would you do that?" Grant asked in shock and amazement.

"I was ordered to distract her, and I found her exotic beauty to be intoxicating. When I offered and she accepted, I was surprised as I did my research and knew she didn't do relationships. Luckily, I planned ahead and brought condoms with me," Jason told him.

"Ok, next question, did you use a condom every single time you two had sex?" Grant asked.

"Of course! I can't afford for my wife to find out I screwed around behind her back; she would kill me, then take me for everything," Jason said.

"Well, your wife is about to find that out, Jason. Seraphina and Ryder were in a car accident, and we found out that she is about eighteen weeks pregnant; that means you're the sperm donor," Grant told him, watching his face closely.

"There's no fucking way I got her pregnant, I had brought three condoms and they were all used," Jason angrily defended.

"And how many times did you two go at it?" Grant asked as he knew what Seraphina told him would be truth. "Think very carefully; either way I am about to beat the living crap out of you, and you aren't going to come out of this on the winning side."

Jason sat back and thought carefully. He was sure he was careful, and he counted the three times during the night, and then realized that their last time was before they got up the morning after. "Oh fuck," Jason said as he realized the last time, they didn't use a condom.

"Exactly; you made a baby with Seraphina; I'm sure she didn't know she was pregnant either as she just agreed to a relationship with Ryder," Grant told him.

"Seriously, she wants a relationship with that man-whore?" Jason spat.

"Well, we've gotten to know him quite well, and not once during the project was he a man-whore. If anything, he was the perfect gentleman. His employees and friends mentioned he stopped all the women-chasing crap when he met Seraphina. They think she might be it for him," Grant told him. "And now, this is where I beat the living shit out of you for treating Seraphina the way you did. Using her and getting her pregnant while you're married. This is going to end your career, and you know it. Sucks to be a greedy bastard, don't it?" Grant said as he stood.

He motioned for Jason to get up as Grant left a twenty on the table for their coffee and followed Jason out. "Oh, I don't think we ever told you this; Seraphina and I served together, so we have some awesome skill sets that will make your eyes bug out of your head," Grant told him, knowing he was trying to plan his escape.

"Now you think I am literally going to beat you, and I really, really do want to do that. Instead, I am going to beat you with brains. It's time to go to your Boss and the Board of Directors for your racing tier; they are going to be very interested in your activities with

Seraphina," he told him, escorting him to the unmarked car while tossing Jason's keys to his buddy who was sitting at a nearby table.

"You can't prove anything," Jason defended.

"Actually, we can; you forget that we had access to everything at your company, and we recently learned how you went far beyond what you were ordered regarding Seraphina. You went rogue, and Mr. Brandon is going ballistic and the Board of Directors for your racing series will also go nuts and likely will fire you, and ensure you never come near the racing scene again. We know the code of conduct you all must sign, and this definitely falls into the category of very bad behavior. Your wife is most definitely going to be pissed at you too," Grant told him, matter of fact.

The drive to Brandon Motorsports was very quiet. Grant had arranged a meeting with Mr. Brandon and the Board of Directors at the same time. He did not want to have to do this twice as he hated to repeat himself. He had Jason exactly where he needed him; he had the documentation and Seraphina's doctor gave him a letter, indicating when she most likely conceived according to the ultrasound they had done.

When they had pulled into the parking lot of Brandon Motorsports, Jason noted a few unknown cars and wondered exactly what he had gotten himself into. He also saw his wife's car in the parking lot, and he felt real fear for the first time ever.

Grant escorted him to the board room as he was told by Sally with Jason following behind him. Jason thought to run as he knew the building better than Grant, but when he looked behind him, saw two people he did not know following them, knew running was not going to get him anywhere.

Grant was feeling smug satisfaction even though he knew he was about to ruin Jason's career. 'He never should have done what he did in the first place.' He thought to himself checking to see two of his friend's trailing behind Jason.

The meeting went exactly as Grant expected; Jason was fired on the spot, and the governing body banned him from the racing series and events. Jason was then ordered by Mr. Brandon to pay Seraphina for damages, as he did not want his company's reputation to be soiled with the allegations that his company had sanctioned Jason having sex, and consequently, getting Seraphina pregnant.

Jason got very angry over that, and a shouting match ensued. But, when Mr. Brandon showed him the court documents he was served that very morning, naming Brandon Motorsports, Mr. Brandon, and Jason Knecht in a lawsuit. All Mr. Brandon wanted was to make it go away as quietly as he could. He could not afford to have anything against his company; they were already teetering on the edge.

The Board of Directors were very interested in that pending court case, and after looking it over and quietly discussing the contents of what they had just learned, decided in one swift motion to strip Brandon Motorsports of its charter and rights to race in the top tiers of the racing community. The Board then ordered Brandon Motorsports, Mr. Brandon, and Jason Knecht to pay for damages done to Seraphina St. Clair and the potential stain to her company that they likely caused.

Grant felt relieved as he knew Sera would stress about what people would say when the world finds out she's pregnant. When he left the building with his small group of friends of his and Sera's, he did feel like justice was served. Greed never got what you wanted, no matter how big the carrot. He looked at the time, and thought he would go and see how Ryder and Sera were doing before he had to go to the airport to pick up his beautiful wife.

Chapter 22

Seraphina woke up feeling like she had been put through the ringer; her head was pounding, her body was hurting in places she did not know existed, and she felt very nauseated and weak. She groaned at the bright lights, and slammed her eyes shut causing more pain to course through her head. She tried to think of why she felt the way she did, but nothing was coming to mind.

"Shh, Seraphina, it's alright, you're safe," she heard a woman say very softly.

"Where am I?" she asked, her voice barely above a whisper.

"You're in the hospital; you and your husband were in an accident," she heard from someone who she assumed was the nurse.

"Where is he?" she asked.

"He had to get some tests done for his concussion," the nurse told her, checking her vitals and such.

"Ok, how long ago was the accident?" Seraphina asked.

"You were brought in over 48 hours ago. You had surgery to repair a tear in your spleen and right kidney; and you have a lot of bumps, bruises, and some cuts from the flying glass. You and baby are doing very well. Your husband was quite upset at how you looked when we brought you into the room yesterday morning," she told her.

"Ok, tell him to wake me when he gets back," she told the nurse before drifting back to sleep.

"Poor thing is exhausted," the nurse murmured as she put notes into the chart that Seraphina had woken up for only a couple of minutes and was confused before going back to sleep.

A couple of hours later, Ryder was wheeled back into the room. He had another scan done on his brain to ensure there was not any bleeding or swelling caused by the accident. He was feeling a little woozy from the sedation they had given him. Once he was settled, he looked over at Seraphina, and noted that there were less tubes and such attached to her, "That has to be a good sign," he said to himself, before closing his eyes.

Later that evening, Grant and his wife, Kelley, peeked into the room where the couple were sleeping, "See? She's fine," Grant whispered to his wife.

"She does not look fine to me," she retorted quietly, visibly worried for her friend. "Who's the guy again?"

"That's Ryder Durand, former client, and soon to be Sera's partner," he told her.

"Ah, cool, is he like the sperm donor too?" she asked.

"No, I took care of that piece of shit. It'll be bad enough when Sera finds out," he told her.

"Well, you better tell her pronto," Kelley said.

"Kelley, shut-up," they both heard softly from inside the room.

Grant quietly snickered as Seraphina had woken up and heard Kelley.

The couple walked into the room, "Hey sweetie, how do you feel?" Kelley asked softly, noting Ryder was still sleeping.

"I feel like hell, and I want someone to just put me out of my misery," she quietly muttered, her eyes still closed. "My head pounding is making me sick."

"That I am afraid is going to happen for a while, you have a concussion. The air bags didn't deploy, so you hit your head a couple of times as the car spun around," Grant told her, taking her hand into his.

"Ugh, this sucks," she muttered. "Oh, who's my husband?"

"What do you mean?" Kelley asked, wondering what she was talking about.

"I remember the nurse or whoever told me my husband and I were in an accident," she said.

"Oh, you and Ryder. They must have assumed you two are married," Grant said softly, looking hard at Kelley.

"Why would they think that?" she asked, her eyes still closed.

"Sera, please sweetie, take it easy, ok? You're pregnant," Kelley told her very softly.

"What?" she asked feeling shocked, opening her eyes to see Kelley, Grant, and Ryder sleeping in the bed next to her.

"Yea, I'm sorry, that bastard Jason got you pregnant; you're about eighteen weeks or so," Grant told her.

Seraphina did not say anything for a while, digesting the information that she was told. "Did he do that on purpose?" she asked, after several long minutes.

"Sera, please, we will talk about this when you're better, ok? Ryder knows too, and he is very worried about you," Grant told her as Kelley gently stroked her hair, soothing her.

"Just kill me now," she muttered very quietly, trying not to puke.

"I will call for the nurse to see if they can give you something," Kelley said quietly.

A few minutes later, a nurse and Dr. Jones came into the room, "Hi Seraphina, can you please tell me how you feel?" the doctor asked her.

She told him exactly what she was feeling, and after he examined her and her chart, "I can give you something to help with the nausea, but it might not go away completely; everything I give you has to be baby safe," he told her.

Seraphina sighed and asked, "What if I don't want the baby?"

"Excuse me?" Dr. Jones asked, wondering if he had heard right.

"Never mind," Seraphina said.

"Sweetie, Ryder wants to take care of you, it's alright," Grant told her, trying to ease whatever was going on in her mind.

Seraphina didn't say anything until after the doctor and nurse left the room, "I don't want any ties to Jason. This baby is his and I can't have this baby," she whispered.

"I already took care of Jason, ok? It's fine, I promise Sera," Grant said.

"I hate that I let my judgement be colored by a desire to want love," she muttered, feeling her tears fall down her cheeks. "I'm going to have to break Ryder's heart too."

"Don't do anything yet. Let's get you healthy before anything goes any further. Besides, if you really don't want this baby, I'll take it," Kelley said, tears springing to her eyes. "I can't seem to get pregnant Sera, and you are, I will take your baby."

"Oh Kelley, I'm sorry," Seraphina said, softly knowing how badly Kelley wanted another baby. "We will get this figured out," pulling Kelley into a hug, letting their tears flow down their cheeks.

Grant was choking up, seeing his wife and best-friend crying, wishing he could wave a wand and make it all better.

While there was a lull in the conversation, Ryder woke up, "Still too damn bright," he softly murmured, closing his eyes against the brightness of the room.

"Sorry Ryder, I'll turn down the lights," Grant told him quietly, going to the panel to lower the lights. "The doc was in here looking at Sera."

Ryder opened his eyes, and looked over, "Hey, sweetheart, good to see you," he said, noting the tear tracks on her cheeks.

"Sure, if you say so," she muttered. "I just want to be put out of my misery."

Ryder got out of bed and went over to Seraphina's, where he climbed in next to her and brought her face to his and gently kissed her before one of his hands went to her belly and rested there. "We will be fine, I promise," he told her softly.

Chapter 23

*I*t was six weeks later when Seraphina had a follow-up appointment from the accident. She needed to be checked to ensure everything healed properly and there weren't any lasting effects from her concussion or surgery. She was waiting in the examination room with Ryder sitting in the chair next to her; he insisted he be with her for the appointment.

Everything was still a little off for her since the accident; she could not explain it, but things just were not in proper alignment would be the best way to describe it. After a few minutes, Dr. Jones came in, "Hello Seraphina, how are you doing today?" he asked.

"I'm doing alright, I guess. Things still feel a little off to me, I can't really explain it," she told him.

"Alright, that has to do with your brain healing. You will feel like that for a little while longer as your head took quite the ride in that car. Ok, let's look at the incisions to make sure those have healed nicely," he asked as she shifted the gown so he could look at her back for the kidney scar and then the other side for the spleen scar. "Those look great; no pink, and they are smooth and hardly noticeable," he said.

"Next, let's check baby before I hand you over to OB-GYN for them to take over care of you and baby," he said, helping her to lay down while the gown went up, and a blanket covered her legs. He measured her belly, and then took the hand-held monitor to listen for the heartbeat. "That's a very good heartbeat," he remarked, hearing a very strong rhythm.

The doctor then felt around her belly, checking how the baby was laying inside her womb, "Alright, baby is still right side up, you are at about 24- or 25-weeks' gestation, so over the halfway mark, which is good as baby will grow, so make sure you are eating right, taking your vitamins, and getting a lot of rest. And, you can now resume having sex, as any potential for hurting your incisions are gone. But please be careful, you both are still dealing with concussions, so do take it easy," Dr. Jones said. "I am now releasing you to the care of OB-GYN and if there are any issues with your head, let me know," he said as he wrote in her chart before leaving.

"That's it?" Ryder asked.

Seraphina snickered, "Pretty much I guess," she replied as she hopped off the table so she could get dressed.

"Here, let me help," he said as he got up to help her, laying out her clothing for her to put back on.

Once she was dressed, Ryder took her hand and walked with her down to where Grant was waiting for them. "When do you have to go home?" he asked her, quietly waiting for the elevator.

"Soon, I think. I've been here much longer than any of us anticipated," she said softly.

"I have loved having you with me you know," he said, leaning in for a kiss.

"I know, me too. It has been nice just hanging in the evenings with no responsibility and taking it easy for a change. It's also something I'm not used too, so it has been a little hard for me," she replied.

"Sweetheart, you don't have to go you know. You can stay with me as long as you want," he told her softly.

She softly laughed, "I know that, but I do have to go home for a little bit and check in with everything. My company is still my company, and I do have to face my responsibilities," she replied.

"This sucks you know," he muttered as the elevator doors opened to let them off on the main floor.

"I am sorry Ryder," she said, not sure what else she could say.

They rode in silence back to Ryder's place; that's where Seraphina, Grant, Kelley and their daughter, Kayla were staying until Seraphina was cleared to travel home.

When they arrived at the house, Seraphina walked in and went to her room. She sat on the bed, not knowing exactly what she should be doing. She knew that Grant would handle their travel back home, so she did not need to worry about that.

After a couple minutes, there was a soft knock on the door, she got up and saw Ryder on the other side, "Hey," she said, letting him into her room.

"Hey sweetheart, let's talk," he said, sitting on the bed with her.

She sighed, "Ok," she agreed.

"I know you have to go home and I'm sure there's a pile of work waiting on your desk for you. I get that. What I need to know is what about you and me? Are we going to be a couple or not?" he asked.

She looked into his eyes, "I don't think I can. I am having someone else's baby and I cannot saddle that on you. This was my mistake, and I have to own it," she said, feeling her heart break. "I have been thinking long and hard about Kelley's offer, and I think I am going to give the baby up to her and Grant; she desperately wants a baby."

"What about me? Don't I get a say in all this?" he asked softly.

"Ryder, I know you didn't sign up for this, and it's really not fair to you. I think you would be so much better off with someone else other than me. Once I have recovered from having this baby, I need to throw myself even harder into my job as I never ever want to make another mistake like I have again. I just can't chance a relationship with you or anyone," she said.

"I don't think that's fair either. You do not even know if we will click or have that connection. You don't know how I really feel about you either," he told her softly.

"Not so long ago, another man told me he had feelings for me, and they were strong. I took a chance and look where it got me. I can't make another mistake in my life; I've already made too many of them," she said, looking at the floor.

"What mistakes have you made? The way I see it, you took a chance, not a mistake, and it's Jason that made the mistake," he told her, taking her hands into his.

She sighed again, wondering if she should tell someone what happened, or continue to hold it within her tightly.

After a few long and awkward minutes, she started, "A long time ago, Grant and I served in the military together, its why we're best friends. We have some cool skill sets, and with my background, I was used a lot to get into enemy camps for intel and such. I blended in so beautifully that no one looked at me and thought I did not fit in because I do. I know the culture, the traditions, the stories, and more," she started, already feeling her throat constrict as the memories that she tried so hard to forget were still as vivid as all those years ago.

"About, hmm, 18 years or so ago, I think, I was dropped into a hot zone in Afghanistan, trying to find Bin Laden. Of course, I fit in, and I was able to collect a lot of information. What I had not counted on, is one of the elders from the village I was in had decided he wanted me for his wife. Village leaders had that ability, taking women for their own. So, late one evening, I was sneaking away to drop the information I had to my team who was watching from a very safe distance and had just finished my drop. I sat there in darkness for a moment, making sure it was safe for me. It was a good thing, as the man had followed me, but lost sight of me and did not know exactly where I was. I waited until he had moved away, then made a beeline to my room, where I made like I had gone out to retrieve one of my scarves I had hanging on the line," she said with a warble in her voice, and tears started to fall down her cheeks. She took a breath and tried to swallow the lump that had lodged in her throat.

"He returned a few minutes later and ordered me to follow him. Of course, I had no choice, so I did, and he led me to his room, where he ordered me to take my clothing off and lay on the bed. I did what I was ordered; as a woman, I had no rights, and if I wanted to stay alive, I had to obey," she choked out, wishing that lump would go away, and feeling Ryder squeeze her hand tightly.

"He took my body several times that night, leaving me quite battered and bruised. That was my first sexual experience, and because I was a virgin, he reveled in that and claimed me to be his wife. The village had a celebration the following night, and it was also the night Bin Laden paid a visit. I was so freaked out, I nearly jumped out of my skin when I saw who it was," she laughed trying to keep her sanity from the memories that were taking over, feeling her fear rise as if she was there in Afghanistan again, and started to shake as she continued telling Ryder what happened all those years ago.

"Here was the terrorist that we've been trying to find, and he was sitting on the other side of that man, who was now my husband. I could not look at him and I remember shaking from being so fucking scared. I needed to do something, but my mind could only focus on who was sitting so close to me," she rasped out.

"I had excused myself from my husband, which he granted with a public kiss. I left to go to the washroom, and there I contacted my team and told them who was at the celebration and to get me the hell out. I needed to get out of there, and I tried so hard to calm myself down so I could return to the celebration and not rouse suspicion."

Seraphina took a few minutes to try and compose herself before continuing. "I returned to my husband who was happy with me; he really was. It was weird, and the village was so happy that the elder had found the perfect wife. I did exactly what a wife would do and remained next to my husband while I waited for the celebration to end," she told Ryder quietly.

"The evening was finally ending, and Bin Laden decided to stay the night. I was so terrified of what could happen, as I hoped to sneak away. My husband offered him my room, as I was to be in my husband's room again, making sure any escape would not be possible."

Seraphina took another few minutes, feeling her body remember everything that happened, and feeling more tears fall, "So," she said as her voice warbled loudly, "while my husband took my body again, my team snuck into the compound. They were supposed to rescue me first, and thought I would be in my room, which was what I had originally hoped. They were surprised to see Bin Laden in my room with a woman they honestly thought was me. The alarm rang within seconds of the team entering the compound, signaling that there were intruders and prevented my husband from continuing. He ordered me to remain as I was while he threw on some clothes to deal with the intruders," she choked out, feeling an even bigger lump form.

"As soon as he left, I got up, grabbed my stuff and ran, trying to escape the compound and meet up with my team," she told him, stopping a sob from escaping her.

Ryder pulled her close, feeling numb at what she was telling him. He had no words and did not know what he could do to help her.

After a few more minutes, "What I did not realize is that someone had followed me to the washroom and overheard my conversation, so my husband already knew before the alarm sounded, and why it happened so quickly. He was waiting for me, and of course caught me. He took me, and punished me," she sobbed out, feeling each scar light with pain at the memory of receiving each one.

"I have several scars on my back, bottom, and hips from him. And once he had his fill of that, he brutally raped me, making sure I would never want another man to ever touch me," she rasped with another sob.

"He did that several times before the village was bombed and I was rescued. A few months later, I discovered I was pregnant, and I did not tell a soul; I couldn't. I was having nightmares of that man, and I felt so defeated." Seraphina said flatly, feeling numb, tears still falling down her cheeks.

"Instead, I took a leave of absence, and had the baby privately, and gave it up for adoption. Because of the trauma, I had to have a C-section, and then I had complications so that added to the whole I'm never getting involved thing," she told him, feeling utterly drained.

"That is why I just can't have any kind of relationships; I just can't manage them, and the one time I think it might be worthwhile, it's not," she finished.

Ryder heard her story, and could not manage any words, feeling such overwhelming, and warring emotions from her story. Instead, he took her face and kissed her passionately; wanting her to feel the love he had for her. "Seraphina, I will always love you, and I think you are more than worthy of a relationship. You deserve to be loved, cherished, and cared for. Let me be that man," he told her, with all the emotion he had for her in his heart.

Chapter 24

The rest of the day was muted and somewhat drab and dreary. Ryder did not know what to do with the information Seraphina disclosed to him and his head was spinning. He was sitting in the family room when Grant walked in, "Hey, are you alright?" he asked, seeing Ryder's face.

"Nope, not really," Ryder started, "Seraphina told me what happened to her in that village; I can't imagine it."

"It happened; unfortunately, she was only 21 or 22 I think; still so young, and fuck, I still hate myself for not saving her from all that shit," Grant said, feeling his own emotions flare from the memory of seeing her beaten and battered.

"How could you have helped?" Ryder asked, wanting to understand.

"Ah, its complicated, but we missed the mark and she suffered for it," Grant said with a sigh, looking up at the ceiling, trying to quell his emotions. "Now, here we are, so many years later, and she still can't let that shit go. She's tried therapy, hypnosis, and other forms to get past it, but it's always there for some reason."

"And now that she's pregnant again, it's really bringing it all back for her," Ryder muttered, closing his eyes leaning against the back of the sofa, feeling tears threatening to spill.

"What do you mean she's pregnant again?" Grant asked, catching what Ryder said, straightening his position.

"Fuck, I'm sorry. She got pregnant by that thing in the village after he took her virginity. She had the baby and gave it up for adoption," Ryder told him, rubbing his face, trying to make sense of his swirling thoughts. "I figured she would have told you this by now."

"Nope, she never said a word to me, maybe Kelley knows though," Grant said thinking. "So that would mean her child would be about 17 then."

"I guess; she didn't give me specifics; and I don't know how to break through her shell to help her realize that I really do want in. I don't care that she's pregnant; I want her," Ryder said.

"Where is Sera now?" Grant asked.

"She wanted a nap after our talk, so she's in her room. I think she's still in shock from the accident and finding out she is pregnant. It's like she can't handle it or something," Ryder said.

"It's because she can't really, she doesn't know how; her own childhood was not that great. She suffered abuse from her parents. Her dad was Syrian, and her mom was aboriginal; making her a unique beauty, but he was traditional, and women were property. Her mom was also abused growing up, something about the residential school system or something, so Seraphina pretty much got the brunt from both," Grant said.

"So, all she knows is abuse, and she's scared to have a kid because of her past?" Ryder asked, starting to put some pieces together.

"I think so," Grant agreed thinking about everything Seraphina had endured. "Sometimes, I don't know what goes on in her head. I do know that her becoming a complete workaholic is her solution to all this shit, as it doesn't give her time to think about it."

"And why she's refused to live," Ryder said, with a sigh. "She'd be perfectly happy ignoring herself until her dying day. I had asked her to think about her funeral, and who would mourn and miss her, and what would be said in her eulogy. She couldn't answer me, and now I get why, her past has not been put to bed, and until she can move past it all, she can never have a fulfilling relationship or life."

Ryder got up after a few minutes and went to Seraphina's room to check on her. As he peeked in, he saw her sleeping and he had an idea, and crawled onto the bed next to her and cuddled into her. He quickly felt his eyes grow heavy as sleep overtook him.

Seraphina woke up much later than she expected; however, she was feeling a little better. "Sleep is the key," she muttered with a snicker.

"Sleep is always the key," she heard from behind her.

She turned to see Ryder on the bed with her, "When did you sneak in?" she asked.

"Oh, I dunno, maybe about an hour or so ago," he said.

"Ah, so you're saying I need more sleep," she said as she snuggled into him.

"Yes, I do say that; you haven't been getting enough sleep for years now. Your body is now protesting and making you rest," he told her, before kissing her temple.

"Yea, I think you're right," she said with a sigh. "I need to slow down, I need to rest for sure, and maybe it's time I took some steps back from the company. I've been working so hard that even with this nap, I'm still exhausted."

"You're going to be tired for some time; let your body heal and especially let your mind heal. I think it will do you so much good," he said softly, stroking her hair.

"And you're going to make me I bet," she replied, snuggling closer.

"I am, and you can't stop me," he replied, bringing her even closer to him. "Everything will be fine. Sera, you have to sometimes let go and let things happen on their own."

She laughed softly at that, "Oh God, like I know how to do that. That's like asking for the championship without competing."

Ryder laughed at the analogy, "If you think so; but so many people are living like that, and I think it would do you a lot of good to reduce your stress, working hours, and other stuff to help you heal. If anything, it won't hurt," he told her.

"Yea, I know," she replied. "Grant said we're going home near the end of the week and when I come back, I don't know yet. It'll depend on how much is on my desk, and how much I can pass onto other team members," she said, shifting to look at him. "I'm not sure how all of this is going to work, but one step at a time, right?"

"Exactly, one step at a time; but you will need to make sure that you remain the priority; sleep, eating properly, and not too much stress, alright?" he said.

"I will try, that's all I can promise," she replied.

"Good; I'll be getting daily reports from Grant," he told her.

"Fantastic," she muttered with a grin, "You got him to the dark side, did you?"

Ryder laughed, "It really wasn't all that difficult. He worries about you and wants to make sure you are not doing too much. Before, I don't think it clicked that you had been working way too hard, but now he knows."

"God, this is so going to suck," she quietly muttered, feeling Ryder snicker.

Chapter 25

$\int$ eraphina had started the task of packing up her stuff for the trip home and had just put on her pajamas after a shower when Ryder softly knocked at the door, "You busy?" he asked her, before stepping into her room.

"Nope, just getting ready for an early evening, why?" she asked.

"Well, if you're up for it, I'd like to take you somewhere," he replied.

"Oh? I'm not dressed and where is this place?" she asked curiously.

"Oh sweetheart, I don't know if you remember, but our date was cut short by a rather unfortunate accident," he told her.

"Yes, I remember," she replied, wondering what he had in mind.

"So, I thought, this evening would be a continuation of that evening," he told her softly.

"Oh, I see. Well then, what did you have in mind?" she asked, as she took his hand.

"Follow me, please," he said, leading her from her room to his room.

When the door opened, there were flowers, candles, and soft music playing in the background. "Well, look at what we have here," she said, walking into the room, and looking about. She turned to face Ryder, seeing him closing the door behind him.

"This is you and I; no one else is allowed, alright?" Ryder said, as he brought over a drink to her.

"I'm not sure what you mean by that," she said, accepting the glass.

"It means that you have to leave all the crap that has happened outside those doors. It means no work, no thinking about other stuff, just you and I," he told her softly.

She looked at him and the seriousness of his face. "I see, I will do my best," she replied, taking a sip. "This is tasty, what is it?"

"It's a blood orange Italian soda," he told her, also taking a sip. "Mmm, that is good," he agreed.

After a few minutes, Ryder put his glass down, and went over to Seraphina, where he took her into his arms, and started a slow dance with her. They slowly moved about the room, waiting for her to relax, and let the atmosphere ease any doubts she may have.

After several minutes, Ryder gently brought her face up to his and kissed her, trying to convey the emotion he had for her. Wanting her to know how much he felt for her, and how much he wanted her to feel the same about him.

He gently broke the kiss and moved to her neck, where she allowed him access, feeling soft lips kiss along her neck that was beginning to fan the flames of her desire.

His own flames were beginning to burn as he continued to kiss along her neck and lips, while slowly guiding her to the bed. When he knew they had reached his bed, he kissed her hard, igniting the desire he knew was brewing inside of her.

When he broke the kiss, she gasped, needing air, "Oh Ryder, you sure know how to kiss," she murmured, as he helped her lay on the bed.

"We are just getting started," Ryder said as he got comfy next to her on the bed.

He brought her close, and encircled his arms around her, cuddling and kissing. He wanted to take his time with her, to make sure she had the best experience possible. He felt her hand begin to roam along his shirt, finding the opening at the collar and sliding her hand in to feel the heat of his skin.

"Mmm, I like that," he murmured softly, before resuming his gentle kissing along her neck. "Your skin is so soft," caressing her arm, feeling the softness before moving his hand to her neck, bringing her face to his, so he could kiss her deeply.

Ryder moved a bit so he could touch more of her body, caressing with gentle touches with his fingers, and lips. He could hear the slight changes in her breathing, learning what she liked so far.

He felt her other hand begin to work underneath the shirt, feeling the soft hair he had on his lower chest, before bringing her other hand to the same place, feeling his warm skin with both hands.

Ryder moved so that he was sitting while she remained lying, and removed his shirt for her, before leaning over her, and kissing her while his one hand worked on the buttons of her night shirt. He was a little nervous that he was moving a little too fast, but, he also had to admit, they had waited a very long time to properly consummate their relationship.

He felt her hands help with the buttons of her shirt, and once they were undone, his hands slid the soft material away to expose her beautiful breasts. "You are so beautiful," he said softly, before moving to worship her breasts; full, large, with erect nipples that were begging for attention.

He gently kissed his way, finding a nipple and taking it into his mouth so his tongue could play with the hardened bud, while his other hand went to the other to gently massage and squeeze, feeling the fullness before he moved his mouth over to the other breast to ensure it had the same attention as its mate.

Seraphina arched her back into Ryder's mouth, feeling the sensations he was giving her, wanting more. "Ryder, god, babe, please," she whispered, wanting more.

"All in good time my love," he whispered against her growing belly, feeling the hardness that was the baby. He had never seen a pregnant woman before, and so far, he loved the curves her body had. He caressed her belly while she watched him, fascinated with how he was touching her.

"You want this baby, don't you?" she asked him suddenly.

He looked at her trying to decide what he should say to her, "It's not that; you are the first pregnant woman I have ever had the pleasure of seeing. It's incredible," he told her as he shifted his body, trying to get comfortable.

"Oh, just take your jeans off already," she told him with a laugh, seeing him fidgeting about.

He grinned, "How did you know?" he asked, amused as he stood up to ditch his jeans.

"All in how you were trying hard not to be noticed that you were uncomfortable," she told him as he returned to the bed, completely naked. "Well, look at you," she murmured, taking in his body, seeing that he was indeed very fit, and every inch the man she had been dreaming about.

Her hands went to his body, feeling the hardness of his muscles before sliding a hand down to his very hard cock. When her hand grazed him, he hissed in pleasure. "Mmm, you do like that eh?" she said as she suddenly sat up and pushed him down on the bed, "my turn to play a little," she said as she sat on his legs.

"Take it easy sweetheart, I don't want you to push yourself," he said, feeling the silk of her pajama bottoms slide along his legs.

"I will be fine, just let me play," she told him as she took him in both of her hands, feeling how hard he was for her, and noted the velvety softness of his skin. She watched his face as she played, gently stroking, and squeezing. She saw pleasure in his face, with his head on the pillow, eyes locked onto what she was doing, his breathing becoming slightly labored.

She moved a little bit, getting comfortable. He opened his mouth to say something when she moved, and sucked his cock into her mouth, causing him to groan loudly instead. "Oh Jesus," he muttered, feeling her mouth on him.

One of her hands moved about his chest, playing with the hair and muscles, while her other hand helped to steady her while she played with him in her mouth, sucking hard, and playing with the tip, before moving her tongue about the length of his cock.

His eyes had rolled into the back of his head, enjoying what she was doing to him. He was unconsciously rocking his hips, as she continued her play time of him. He tried to stop her before something happened, but she batted his hands away as she worked harder to bring him the orgasm his body craved, with waves of pleasure washing over him.

He moaned her name as she continued to play with his now over sensitized cock, making him squirm and try even harder to make her stop, "please baby," he begged, as he finally brought her up and off him. "I desperately need to please you now so I can recover some bones, at least," he told her as he laid her down where he had been, and hooked the waistband of her pajama bottoms, sliding them down her smooth legs.

"Wow are you gorgeous," he said, taking in her body, her skin, slightly flushed with excitement, while her breasts heaved as she panted. He was drinking up the sight of her and was about to move in when the movement of her belly caught him. He stopped and watched for a moment, watching the baby within move about, "Holy shit," he mumbled as he placed a hand gently on her belly, feeling the baby.

"I do want a baby with you," he said suddenly, looking into her eyes. "I want that whole package of loving wife and kids with you."

As soon as he said it, he knew he killed the mood. 'Dammit' he thought to himself.

Chapter 26

After a few minutes of silence, "One day, maybe," she said to him. "This baby is not ours; it's been promised to Kelley and Grant."

He sighed, "I know, it just hit me that I am so very much in love with you, and I want to watch your body change as you grow our baby," he said softly.

"One day," she told him. "You have to be patient, alright?" she said as she sat up to grab his face with both hands and kissed him hard. "You and I haven't even had sex yet; don't put the cart before the horse," she said, causing him to laugh.

"God, you're right," he said, kissing her before gently pushing her back down so he could begin his playtime.

"I want this to be perfect for you," he murmured, before he kissed her belly while his hands slowly ran up and down her legs, feeling the smooth skin. He continued to caress her as he moved over to where he wanted to be the most.

He moved so that he was between her feet, and slowly moved his way up caressing and kissing along his way so that he would find her ready for him, to bring her as much pleasure as she did him.

He listened to her soft noises of desire as he moved about her body, wanting her to feel how much he felt for her. He knew this was real, and he also wanted to erase all the bad shit that happened to her; recently and in her past. He wanted her to think only of their future together, and the happiness they could have as they progressed with their relationship.

Ryder figured she had enough of the sweet torture as she moaned in frustration as he avoided the place he wanted to explore the most. He waited a moment, and watched her, waiting. She opened her eyes to see a grinning Ryder, "Dammit, do something already," she quietly growled at him.

Ryder snickered at her demands as he lowered himself so he was comfy, as he planned on staying where he was for some time.

He heard her suck in a breath when she felt his breath on her inner most folds. He waited a moment, taking in her wetness and beauty before he gently took her delicate flesh into his mouth, bringing a long moan from her.

He gently sucked, rolled, licked, and tickled her, creating sensations of desire, and hearing her noises of need. "Oh baby, you are so amazing," he said to her, barely able to see her face above the belly. He moved a bit so he could introduce more sensations for her.

"Ryder, please, oh please," he heard her quietly beg. He knew she was beginning that climb towards bliss, and he quickened his pace a little bit, moving a little faster with his mouth and hands, wanting her to find that amazing place of ecstasy.

He wanted to watch her as she came apart, so he adjusted his position so he could still have his hands and mouth on her, while watching her face. He felt her growing hotter, and her noises became louder, as she grabbed the sheets, needing an anchor, while her body shook with the impending explosion that was about to spread through her entire body.

Ryder worked just a little harder, moving his other hand to rub her hardened clit, while his other hand slid about her breasts. Just when he thought she needed more, she exploded with pleasure. He could feel her entire body throb rhythmically, as she panted and moaned loudly through her orgasm.

He continued to play with her clit, gently bringing her many aftershocks to course through her body. He saw how flushed her body became, and the thin sheen of sweat that instantly popped out on her body, as her breathing was still erratic.

She took a long time to finally float back to the bed as Ryder kept her body aroused, with need. "Please stop," she quietly begged, "I can't take anymore."

"Oh sweetheart, you are so beautiful, and there's still more to come tonight," he said as he moved so that he was lying next to her.

"Oh, I don't know if I have the bones for that," she said.

"Now you know how I felt after what you did to me," he told her, gently kissing her neck.

Seraphina snickered, "So that was payback?"

Ryder looked at her for a moment, "No, but I want you to know what you do to me," he told her as he moved over her, settling between her legs, making sure she was comfortable.

She watched him as he arranged them so they could finally join their bodies, while making sure her and baby would not be hurt. "You, are, amazing," he said as he very slowly slid into her wanting body, feeling her intoxicating heat, and incredible tightness sheath his cock as he continued to slide in.

He watched her face, and all he saw was pleasure radiating from her as she felt him slide home. "Oh god, Ryder," she murmured quietly. He completely filled her, feeling the tightness of her own body, and feeling his every pulse within her.

"You are exquisite, and perfect," he whispered to her as he started to move within her, creating that delicious friction they both needed.

She reached out to him, grabbing his hands that were holding her legs in place as he started to move a little faster and harder, "oh yes," she chanted, as he did exactly what she needed.

Ryder felt her grow hotter as he moved, and the sensations were causing him to lose his concentration and abandon any control he had, as his body demanded so much more. He shifted Seraphina as he started to pound into her with abandon, hearing their skin slapping together and hearing her chanting softly.

His growl started very quietly and low, but as he barreled towards that much needed release, his growl grew as did his need to feel her come apart around him, "Baby, give it to me," he growled, as he felt her body contract, gripping his cock even tighter.

He heard her and opened his eyes to see her body instantly flush, with a flood of liquid that he felt surround him and run down his legs and balls. That feeling brought him to his release as he growled, spilling deeply within her, feeling her throb, as he throbbed within her.

Both were somewhere else other than the planet, and it took them some time to regain their senses. Ryder realized that he was not as considerate as he wanted to be with her. He was scared that he may have hurt her with his needs.

"Sorry love," he whispered as he stayed still within her.

"For what?" she asked, still not quite back to earth.

"I lost my self-control, and," he said trying to control his breathing, "I was much rougher with you than I wanted to be."

"Ryder, I loved what you did to me; it was amazing," she told him, looking into his eyes. "You can do that to me anytime you want."

"Oh babe, I am in love with you," he whispered as he slid out of her, feeling the loss, and moving so he lay next to her.

"I think I'm in love with you, too," she told him, before moving in to kiss him.

Chapter 27

*T*his Thursday morning, Seraphina had to return home; she had not been in her home for what seemed like forever, and she knew that there were some things that would need her attention. Ryder was not happy she was leaving. He knew that she would be back, but that was not improving his mood any.

He knew that he needed to concentrate on his last year of racing, his company, and all he wanted was Seraphina. He knew he found what he had been looking for in her, and he would do everything he could to ensure she was happy, safe, loved, and cherished.

Today, he had to drive them to the airport before he left for the track. He was hoping to show her off before they left, but she wanted to keep her pregnancy quiet, therefore avoiding the racing scene until she was ready. He sighed, wishing he could help her understand that he didn't care she was pregnant. Instead, he knew he had something amazing with her; their recently new sex life could attest to that.

Seraphina was getting tired of being teased by Grant. He had overheard the couple a few times and would then tease her about it like an annoying brother would. Ryder was amazed that Grant could tease her the way he did and not be six feet underground. Kelley had to step in to ensure her husband remained alive, as she knew Seraphina was coming close to killing Grant.

At the airport, Ryder waited for them to finish checking in and drop off their luggage. They had some time before they had to go through security. They walked about the airport, finding a coffee shop to sit in for a little bit. Ryder was having difficulty; he did not want her to go, plain and simple. No one was paying attention to their surroundings and had not picked up that a few other people were interested in Ryder and his new girl.

Soon enough, it was time for Seraphina, Grant, Kelley, and their daughter to make their way through security so they could catch their flight. As they walked towards the security entrance, Ryder had a firm grip on her hand, not wanting to let her go.

"I will be back before you know it," she told him quietly, trying to quell his fears.

"I know, I just wish you didn't have to go is all," he told her as she turned to face him.

"This time away will go fast, alright? You have a lot of work to catch up on as do I, and you want your last year of racing to be awesome. Concentrate on that, and before you know it, I'll be back here with you," she told him, moving her hand to stroke his cheek.

Ryder sighed as he looked into her eyes, "I love you Sera," he said, before capturing her lips in a kiss.

"I love you as well, so make sure you stay out of trouble," she said to him, when they broke the kiss.

Meanwhile, there were a few people who were watching from a distance, very interested in the display of Ryder and Seraphina, and had taken a couple of photos to sell. One photo showed a baby bump on Seraphina as Ryder had absently rubbed her belly as he kissed her.

"Ok, I have to go, you, please be good alright? I don't know if I will have enough bail money for you," she told him, teasing him.

"Ha; I am much too old for that kind of crap, besides, the only person I want to get into that kind of trouble with is busy," he told her.

"Oh? Who's that?" she asked him.

"You; you're going to be busy working, and stuff. No time for me," he tried to say sadly, but she caught the grin he was trying to hide.

"Uh huh, please just stay out of trouble?" she softly pleaded with him. "And now, I must go, or I might miss the flight. Wait, you want me to miss the flight, don't you," she said, narrowing her eyes at him.

"Of course, I want you to miss the flight, and then you can stay with me," he told her, before he kissed her long and hard, "I love you, stay safe and call me when you get home," he told her.

"I love you, and I will," she replied, as she broke from his embrace to go through security.

Ryder stood there, watching her disappear through the crowd of others also trying to get through security, "This sucks already," he mumbled to himself.

When he lost sight of her, he turned to leave the airport so he could go to his own plane. The season was still in the early weeks; even though he started his season late because of his concussion. Now he needed to focus so he could at least get a win or two, "Maybe the championship too," he said to himself, thinking that would be an awesome send-off for his career.

While he was deep in thought, he was not paying attention to others around him and hadn't seen some of the media people that were routinely at the tracks in the airport as well. It was something he should have thought of, as it was travel day for most people who needed to be at the track, but he was so focused on Seraphina, it just never occurred to him.

When Ryder arrived at the track, he first checked in with his teams, making sure everyone and everything arrived without issues. He worked on some emails and such before leaving the transporter to go to his motorhome for the evening. When he walked out, there were a handful of media people there waiting to talk to him. At first, he was wondering what he did to garner the attention. When a media person pulled up the photo already going viral on social media, of he and Seraphina, kissing, and her belly plainly visible, it dawned on him that he was not more careful protecting her from them.

He looked at them, formulating what he could say that would not hurt Sera, "I have found love with an amazing woman; please let us have the privacy we need so our relationship can continue," he asked them.

One media person asked about her baby bump. "We are not talking about our private lives at this time, and you aren't going to get any information," Ryder said, trying to steer them away from her.

"Look," Ryder said, getting frustrated already at their constant questions, "leave her alone; she is very busy and works very hard. She had to go home to attend to business. She and I have something that we want to continue to explore and let grow; maybe we will get married, maybe we will have kids, but at this time, it's our business, not yours. And, I am not going to say anything more about our relationship," he said as he proceeded to walk away from the media.

"Fuck," he swore as he let himself into his motorhome. "All I need is someone to put this all together, and Sera could get hurt over this shit," he muttered to himself. He rubbed his face while trying to think; 'who would want this information?' he thought.

"Jason knows, and Brandon Motorsports are no longer allowed to compete, is there anyone who would want to hurt her just for spite?" he asked himself, thinking.

Chapter 28

*T*he weeks flew by as Seraphina continued to work on her company; she was now at the 33-week mark in her pregnancy and was told that travel was no longer allowed. She snickered when Dr. Bear told her this, and he asked her why.

"My partner is in North Carolina, and he was hoping I could go for a couple of weeks. Sucks to be him; if he wants to see me, then he has to come here," she told the doctor.

"Ah, I see. Will he be in the delivery room with you?" Dr. Bear asked.

"I don't know; I don't think he thought that far ahead," she said, thinking about it.

As she sat on the sofa later that night, she thought back to what Dr. Bear asked her. She had promised this baby to Kelley and Grant, and she was more than happy to give the baby over to them. The baby she wanted to keep was the one she truly wanted and planned for. Her two babies were unplanned, and she did not want ties to her past mistakes. She thought back to her first pregnancy, and the hell she had gone through. She had made her decision quickly to give it up for adoption, as she did not want a child that constantly reminded her of how it was conceived, through rape. "There was no way I was mentally or even physically capable of raising a child," she said to herself, getting up to get some more tea. "It took me years to finally put him and what he did behind me. Thank god he's dead, and likely rotting in hell," she said, as she sat back down.

She then thought back to the one relationship she did have before swearing off all men, "Geez, I haven't thought of him in years. Wonder what he's up to these days," she said, thinking of Steve; a kindred spirit, lover, and air force pilot. "He was so much fun; but when I found him like that, damn," she recalled, thinking back to that day when she had arrived home early from deployment as she was injured in an IED explosion. She found him in their bed, having way too much fun with three different women, at the same time. She was so shocked at the scene before her, that it took her a moment to realize they had stopped their play time, and Steve was trying to gain her attention. She threw him and his lady friends out by throwing their clothing out the window. As soon as he left, she had the locks changed, and had a mutual friend come and box his stuff.

Grant was so mad at himself that she got hurt and no one else did on that last deployment. She had shrugged it off, saying she was the one who took the jump from the vehicle setting it off. She was not seriously injured; but the shocks were enough to cause some permanent damage to her back and hips, as they became dislocated when she finally landed. It was after that she retired and did not look back. She took some time for herself, to heal, and figure out what she wanted to do next.

Consulting was a natural fit for her. She knew strategy, how pieces fit together, and how to make things work the way she wanted them to. After serious consideration, and working for a few idiot consulting firms, she started her own business. "Ha, those jerks had no idea what I was capable of," she murmured, thinking back to her former boss. "Best decision I ever made."

She was still deep in thought when her phone rang. She picked it up without looking at who would be calling her, at this time of night, it was usually Ryder. "Good evening, what's up?" she said.

"Is this Seraphina?" a woman's voice asked.

"No, this is her assistant; how can I help you?" she asked, instantly on guard, her mind racing.

"I was hoping to talk with Seraphina, when will she be available?" the woman asked.

"Well, that depends, are you a client of ours?" Seraphina asked, trying to figure out who it was.

"No, I'm not a client; but we do have a mutual friend that I would like to talk with her about," the woman replied.

"Alright; she is very busy with clients right now. Could I please have your name and number, and I will have her call you as soon as she's available, which will most likely be tomorrow," Seraphina said, hoping to get more information from the woman.

"Sure, that would be great; my name is Brea Knecht, and my number is, 916 555 9099," she told her.

"Brea, thank you, I will make sure that she gets the message, and contact you tomorrow," she replied before hanging up.

As soon as that conversation was done, Seraphina opened her laptop and started to search for the name and phone number. While she waited for a hit, Ryder called her.

"Hey babe, how's it going?" he asked her.

"A whole lot is going; do you know who a Brea Knecht is?" she asked him.

"I think so, isn't she Jason's wife? Why are you asking about her?" he asked, wondering what was going on.

"She just called me wanting to talk to me," she told him.

"What? What did she say?" he asked, immediately concerned for her.

"I told her I was my assistant, and I would call her tomorrow; in the meantime, I'm doing a search on her." She replied, seeing some information fill the screen.

"She's still married to Jason? Holy shit," she said, as she saw her profile load. "I thought she would have dumped his ass when she found out what he did. And she is half his age too, wow, cradle robber," she muttered. "Poor thing."

"Hey, please be careful; if she found out that you're having a baby could complicate things for you, and I don't want you getting hurt," he told her, worried.

"Yea, I know, and I can tell her straight up it isn't his if she thinks that," she said.

"I don't know sweetheart, I don't like this," he told her.

"Well, I can't go anywhere until after the baby is born, and I'm sure she has no idea where I am, so I think I will be alright," she told him.

"You can't come see me?" he asked, feeling a little put out as he really wanted some time with her.

"Ryder, there's like six or seven weeks left for this baby to bake; of course, I can't go anywhere! What if I were to go into labor early? You want to talk about complicating things, that would be a hell of a complication," she told him. "Oh, are you going to be in the delivery room with me and the rest of the crew?" she asked him, suddenly changing directions.

"I don't know; I hadn't thought about it. Do you want me there?" he asked, as he didn't want to intrude on something, she may not want him to witness.

She thought for a moment; "I don't know; Kelley and Grant will be there as will Kayla, the nurses and doctor. Hell, that's already six people," she said with a snicker. "What's one more, helping me through this? Besides, you'll get some practice for when your future wife has a baby."

"True, practice makes perfect," he replied. "Ok, I will be your way in another week as we do the tracks in your area; so, I should get some quality time with you," he told her.

"You just want to get laid," she teased him.

"Uh, yea! Making love with you is my favorite activity," he told her.

"Ah, I see, I did not know that" she said with a laugh. "In the meantime, I am going to do a little research and find out what she's after, and from there I can set my action plan," she told him, with a large grin.

"Please be careful love; I can't have anything happen to you, alright?" Ryder said, seriously.

"I am always careful, you know this, please don't worry too much about me? I have Grant who will kill anyone who tries to hurt me," she told him softly, trying to ease his worry.

"Doesn't mean I'm not going to worry," he told her. "I love you Sera."

"I love you, and I will be careful, I promise," she told him.

Chapter 29

The next day, Seraphina had prepared herself to talk to one Brea Knecht and find out what she wanted. She had gotten some information general stuff though; she had never gotten into trouble, so no file like that, and other than the usual identification records, she was squeaky clean.

At around ten that morning she made the call to Brea, feeling slightly nervous and anxious about all the 'what ifs' that were going through her mind as she waited for Brea to answer the phone. She made sure that her number was blocked, figuring she had been snooping and came across her number in Jason's phone.

"Hello?" Brea answered.

"Hello Brea, I am Seraphina St. Clair, I understand that you called last night and wanted to speak with me, what can I do for you," she said very professionally.

"Hi, thank you so much for calling me back. I am hoping that you can help me with an issue I am having regarding Jason Knecht," she started.

"What is that?" she asked.

Brea sighed, "I understand that he seduced you as part of his job; is this true?" she asked.

"It is unfortunately; I made a very serious error in judgment as Jason was incredibly charming," she said to her.

"Yea, I so get that. I am so sorry that happened to you," Brea said. "God, I just don't know what to do."

"What do you mean?" Seraphina asked cautiously, but curious at the same time.

"He lost his job, and he can't find a job with the other race teams. No one's willing to take a chance on him, so it seems he will never work in the industry ever again. I'm fine with that, as I'm sure there are other jobs he can do, but he's been..." she dropped off.

"He's been what?" Seraphina softly prompted.

"He's been, I don't know, seriously depressed and very mad, and I can't seem to make him understand that he made the choice that ended his career as the way he described what he did as just a business transaction, and that made me sick. It made me think about why he would do that to anyone, and so, well, I just wanted to talk to you a bit and learn a little about you. I am afraid that he might be planning something against you," she told her.

"Ah, I see. Well, he's been warned about trying to come after me as I am very well protected by many people and layers of government," she told Brea. "I am a little worried about you, however, are you still with him?"

Brea sighed, "For now, yes; I found out a few months ago that I'm pregnant and I'm scared about having this baby alone," she said shyly.

"Oh, I see. You do not have to stay with him if you really don't want to; there are organizations and people who are trained to help. I'm sure you have family that would love to help you," she said softly.

"My mom has been working hard to convince me to leave him. I just never thought Jason was like that, and I'm at a loss as to what to do just now," Brea said.

"I understand, and I am sorry that you were caught in something you were never prepared to deal with. This must be very hard for you. Whatever you decide, I'm sure will be the decision that's right for you, whatever that may be," Seraphina said softly.

"I'm leaning towards leaving him, I just don't know if I have the strength to divorce him and have a baby at the same time," Brea said, feeling a little defeated.

"That is something only you can answer, so, I will say this, take the time to think through everything and think ahead to your own future. What do you see? What are your hopes and dreams, and what do you have to do to achieve them?" she asked softly. "Don't let Jason or anyone else push you into something you know in your gut you don't want. Do what's right for you."

"Yea, and that's what I am trying to do. I just needed to hear from you to make sure that what Jason said isn't true and what I heard from my dad is," she said. "My dad was at that meeting the day everyone found out how Jason seduced you, and he I think was madder than I was. Thank you for your time, you have helped me a lot; and I hope you and the baby are doing well."

Seraphina was slightly shocked that she brought up the baby, "Thank you; Ryder and I are very excited about this baby," she said after a moment.

"It's not Jason's baby?" Brea asked, surprised.

"No; Ryder and I created this precious baby. I didn't know I was pregnant until we were in an accident a few months ago," she told her.

"Wow; I thought it was Jason's as he boasted that he got you pregnant," Brea said.

"No; he had used a condom every time, and Ryder and I made a little mistake, but we are so happy the baby happened; he's so excited about the baby," she told her.

"Wow, that's awesome, I'm happy for the both of you," Brea said before hanging up.

"Holy shit, I still don't know what that was about," she said to herself after a few minutes. She sat there and thought about the conversation she had.

'She is young; very young, and I bet quite scared and unsure of herself by what happened. Her happy little world imploded, and her husband is not who she thought he was, and then add a pregnancy..., poor thing is lost and in need of something to cling to. Oh, I hope her mother can persuade her to leave that bastard. She does deserve better.' She thought to herself as she prepared for a meeting with a new client.

This client had asked to meet her in her offices as they did not want word of a consulting firm to spread through the company before they even decided if they wanted to hire her. She had a few clients that would introduce her to the company after they had been hired to do a job. Sometimes, that was what worked, and sometimes, it backfired.

"I'm meeting that potential client in the boardroom now," she said to Grant as she walked past his office door.

"Have fun," she heard him reply with a snicker.

"Thanks for having my back," she yelled back at him, hearing him laugh loudly. "One day, I should make him meet new clients for a change."

As she walked towards the board room, she wondered which way this client would go. "God, I need an agreeable and easy client for a change; I'm exhausted after the last three I've had to deal with," she muttered to herself as she walked into the board room.

The client had his back to the door, looking out the window and had not heard her come in, "Hello, I'm Seraphina St. Clair," she to the person waiting for her in the board room. When the person turned to face her, she became frozen in place as the person before her was Jason Knecht. "What the fuck are you doing here?" she demanded as soon as she managed to regain her composure, feeling fear wash over her while going to sit in her chair, and pressed the security button located under the table at the chair only she was allowed to sit in. She desperately hoped they would flood in the room in seconds.

"I am here to get back what was taken from me," he said with anger clearly written on his face.

"You were fired because you were a greedy bastard who didn't care who he hurt in the process," she said as she stood again, going towards the bank of cupboards behind her chair to get some water hoping to stall for a minute waiting for security.

"I lost my job because you let me fuck you," he spat.

"You lost your job because you wanted something you shouldn't have as the spoiled child you are," she replied to him, turning to face him, her belly very visible to him.

"Holy fuck, you really are pregnant?" he asked, changing the direction of his conversation while his eyes focused solely on her large belly.

"Yes, I am, and I have been busy preparing for the arrival with Ryder," she told him, seeing his demeaner change as she slowly moved her hand behind her, looking for her personal handgun she kept in the drawer.

"What if I want your baby?" he asked carefully.

"What about the baby you made with Brea?" she countered, trying to redirect his attention.

"Brea said it's not mine," Jason told her, his eyes still on her belly not realizing that Seraphina knew of his wife and her pregnancy.

"Oh, I bet it is yours and she's hurt that you screwed around on her." Seraphina told him, "she's very young, and doesn't understand how a man like you could be so selfish," she told him finding the gun, sliding it out, and moving it to her back pocket.

"I think I want your baby," Jason said, looking up at her face, his demeanor visibly different, and his face showing him to being a little crazed. "I know it will be incredibly gorgeous with your genes and will remind me of you."

"Jason, you don't get to decide this," she said, wondering where the hell her security detail was, they were never this slow, and she was beginning to feel panic overwhelm her as she realized Jason was no longer in his right frame of mind.

She moved to sit so she could press the button again, "Don't bother, I disabled your security button. As far as they know, you are safe, happy, and not in any danger," he told her. "I will have that baby even if I have to rip it out of you."

"You will not have this child; it isn't yours in the first place," she said, looking him in the eye.

"That's bullshit," he spat, looking even more crazed, like something had snapped in him.

"It's not; I had spent a night prior to you with Ryder in my room; it's his," she told him, hoping to throw him off long enough to figure out a plan of action, as she made note of where everything was in the room, what had been moved and where he was standing, and how he was moving, knowing full well she couldn't move nearly as fast as she would need to.

"Fuck off; you let Ryder fuck you before me?" he spewed, moving towards her like the predator he was and she the prey.

"You never asked why he wanted to see me that night; I would have told you," she said, standing again and moved opposite of his moves.

"Oh, I am liking this game. You get me hot," Jason said, moving towards her as she moved away from him.

"Jason, I am tired of all this bullshit; go home and drown your sorrows in a bottle of Jack," she said as she had the door within a few feet of her and wanting desperately to get away from him.

"Ah, no, it's you babe; as soon as I had your tight body, it's all I've been craving since that night," he told her as he figured out her plan. "You can run, but I will have you," he said as he lunged, making a move towards her.

Seraphina made for the door as he grabbed her and flung her against the wall. She took a moment to clear her head and regain her balance, so she did not fall as she felt her panic rise, and her body begin to shake from all her other memories of trauma, as she focused on him walk towards her, with a knife out. "I am getting that baby now, too bad your beautiful body will be wrecked," he said as he got ready to attack her.

Just as he made like he was going to cut open her belly, her trembling hand found her gun and fired, without taking aim at him, surprising him as he felt something hit him. He stopped and looked at his side, seeing blood begin to stain his shirt. "You fucking bitch, you ruined my shirt," he yelled as she saw him lunged at her again, this time the knife making contact with her skin.

She screamed as loud as she could as she fired her gun again, hoping she hit him somewhere critical. She suddenly felt very dizzy as her body went numb hearing Jason's scream of pain in the distance.

She needed to sit and allowed gravity to set her body down on the ground as she saw Grant and her security detail enter the board room in slow motion.

Grant took one look at Seraphina and the client she was meeting. He instantly felt an anger he had never known until now, and as he walked past Jason, punched him as hard as he could breaking his nose and jaw as he continued towards Seraphina.

"Fuck I'm so sorry, shit Sera, stay with me babe, stay with me," he told her as he tried to stem the flow of blood.

Seraphina felt like everything was in super slow motion now as Grant walked towards her, saying something she could not make out. She also felt like she was no longer in her own body as she did not feel pain anymore. "Sorry," she said, before she lost consciousness.

Chapter 30

Seraphina woke up feeling like she wanted to puke. She was feeling dizzy, and her body felt so heavy, like she was encased in rock, that she could not move. She groaned, trying to make herself move. "Shh, it's alright," she heard Kelley say. "Don't panic, all is well."

It took Seraphina several minutes to gain enough consciousness to figure out something happened. "What happened?" She asked in a whisper, unable to raise her voice beyond that.

"You're going to be ok Sera, I promise. That shithead, Jason attacked you." Kelley said as she texted Grant to let him know Seraphina had woken up, before gently taking her hand and gently squeezing it.

"I don't remember," she whispered, feeling panic rise within her at hearing that name.

"Oh sweetie, it's alright; don't push it ok?" Kelley told her, trying to keep her calm by gently rubbing her head, and squeezing her hand.

"How long" Seraphina asked after a few minutes, trying to process everything.

"Uh, well," Kelley started.

"Fuck, that long huh?" Seraphina said, figuring it had been some time ago.

"Yea; but you're ok, and your body is healing really well," Kelley said, hoping to ease her worry.

"Anything else?" She asked.

"Well, baby is here, doc says seven weeks early," Kelley said quietly, trying not to cause stress.

What?" Seraphina said opening her eyes, "Fuck that's bright." She muttered, closing her eyes again feeling pain course through her body.

Kelley sighed, "Jason managed to stab the side of your belly, causing some awesome bleeding according to Grant. He was so freaked by what he saw, he was really terrified he was losing you and the baby. Once you were brought to the hospital, the ultrasound showed your body had started labor and the knife missed the baby completely, but had hit an artery which is why you were bleeding the way you were." Kelley told her gently, knowing she needed to know, but not wanting her to freak out.

"You were taken for surgery to repair the artery, and baby was delivered by C-Section. He is in the NICU where he is doing well. His lungs are not quite developed yet, so he needs to stay there for a bit longer; but he's gorgeous Sera. He looks exactly like you," Kelley told her. "I don't know if I can take your baby Sera, I think he's meant to be yours."

"I promised you, and I intend to keep my promise," she murmured as she felt sleep creep in again, over the pain she felt.

Seraphina woke up feeling less like she wanted to puke which she thought was good, but she still was not feeling well, "Fuck me," she mumbled.

"Hey sweetheart, take it easy love," she heard Ryder say.

"Please just put me out of my misery," she muttered very quietly, wanting to end all this pain she was feeling.

"I'm glad you're still here with me, love," he told her, kissing her forehead before taking her hand into his.

"What happened?" she asked him.

"That fucker Jason surprised you, and attacked you in your own company boardroom. He somehow managed to disable your security alarm, and then took a stab at you causing some damage. You shot him twice, and somehow, he fell and broke his nose and jaw when he hit the floor. He is at another hospital with cops waiting for him to be released so he can be charged and go to jail. The psychologist thinks he's jumped off the sane wagon," Ryder told her softly, still feeling immense anger. "He's completely lost it, so, I imagine he will be locked up for a very long time to come.

When Grant called him and told him what happened, he nearly had a heart attack. He remembered his body and mind going numb as Grant told him about Jason, and what he did to Seraphina, catching the panic in Grant's voice, before a large wave of anger overtook him; all because that bastard Jason nearly took the one thing he needed in life from him.

"Shit, no wonder I feel like crap," she mumbled, bringing Ryder back to her.

"I know love; I am so happy that you're going to be fine," he said, lifting her hand and kissing it. "When Grant called me to tell me what happened, I freaked. I thought I was going to lose you to that madman, and I was in such a panic, my crew chief did not know what to do, or anyone else really. I felt so many emotions all at once, and the only thing I could focus on was you, and how I nearly lost you," he whispered against the hand he had been kissing, feeling tears sting his eyes as he remembered those feelings.

"Well, I am still here, so there's that," she said, finally opening her eyes, "Ugh."

"Hey, there's your beautiful eyes," he said, stroking her hair. "When your body has healed enough, you'll be allowed to go home."

"Good, I hate hospitals," she said, trying to move a bit to get a little more comfortable. She moved a hand from one side and grazed her belly to try and help herself shift when she felt the lack of a belly. "Ryder, what happened to the baby?" she asked, starting to feel panic rise as she felt around her now soft belly.

"Shh, calm down, he's fine. He had to come early because of what happened; he is in the NICU unit and doing amazing. He's gorgeous babe; all you," he told her softly, trying to ease her fears and prevent her from panicking.

"Shit, poor thing," she said.

"Kelley says she can't take the baby from you," he told her softly.

"But he's hers," she tried to protest.

"No, my love," he said quietly, taking her hands and squeezing them tightly while kissing her forehead. "He is definitely your baby. Stop running and embrace this Sera. Name me as the baby's father, I will raise him with you darling," he said, trying to make her understand. "Maybe you should see him, then you will understand."

"I don't want to see the baby, he belongs to Kelley," she tried again, wanting separation from her mistakes, her go-to and wall of separation for so many years.

"Go to sleep my love; we will talk about this when you've had more rest," he said gently, stroking her hair, helping her to fall asleep.

Once she was asleep, Ryder left her room, to find Kelley and Grant walking towards him. "She's just gone back to sleep," he told them.

"Good; is she still confused?" Kelley asked.

"A little less, but she's insistent that you have the baby," he told them. "And she doesn't want to see the baby at all."

"Maybe once her brain is less muddled from the meds she's on, she will begin to understand," Grant said. "She doesn't tolerate drugs well."

"Right; damn, sorry Ryder, I forgot; some medications don't do well with her, and hell, she won't remember anything once that crap is completely out of her system either," Kelley told him.

"Hey, I'm in this for the long haul. I need her to know this and its fine, we will get through this. I just wish she'd remember that she and I made love before that bastard had her," Ryder said wistfully.

"Wait, what? Are you Serious?" Grant asked, surprised at Ryder's revelation.

"The first night after I finally signed the contract, I had dinner brought in during our meeting and afterwards, we were in her room kissing and such, she kicked me out before anything further happened." Ryder told them.

"After you were delayed, we went for dinner again and afterwards, we went back to her room and were having drinks. She told me she had a thing for me and had to find out," he told them.

"I had to leave early the next morning as something happened at the shop; I left her to sleep knowing she needed it. Maybe she thought she was dreaming with me as she never mentioned it." Ryder said, thinking and beginning to understand why she had not confronted him about their night together.

"That must suck; I am sorry Ryder. If I had known, I would have made sure that she would have remembered and would have taken better care of herself. She sometimes has memory issues if she takes something to help her sleep, or maybe in your case, had some drinks, and she did that night, she likely won't remember," Grant said, "she is quite the lightweight when it comes to alcohol."

"That so makes sense to me, and why you never chased anyone, except her; you've been in love with her the day you met her, right?" Kelley asked.

"I have, the minute I saw her I fell in love," Ryder confirmed.

"Remember Steve?" Kelley asked Grant, turning to face him.

"Yea, why?" he asked.

"Who's Steve?" Ryder asked.

"Steve was a man she had lived with before she came home injured from her last deployment, and found that yahoo in bed with several women having the most amazing time, I'm told," Kelley said.

"Ok, so?" Grant said.

"He thought he loved her, but never wanted children, like Sera in those days. They were good for each other, but she needed a love that had actual depth, and unknowingly found it with Ryder, but confused it with Jason. Delayed reactive timing is a thing, and Seraphina always takes her time thinking through stuff. She could have confused Ryder and Jason, and not known it," Kelley told them.

"Yup, because she confused Steve with the other guy she should have chosen," Grant said, thinking way back, beginning to put the pieces together.

"Exactly! Ryder, she is so in love with you; just wait and see. In the meantime, the hospital needs information for the baby. I am willing to bet that he belongs to you and Seraphina, so, complete the paperwork with you as the father and she the mother of course. Name him, and I know she will put the pieces together once her muddled brain has ditched those drugs she's on," Kelley told him.

"I have no idea what to even name the little guy," Ryder said, suddenly feeling scared and overwhelmed.

"If you had a son, what name would make you smile and get those warm fuzzy feelings?" Grant asked him.

Ryder was so deep in thought, that he did not notice Grant and Kelley had left him. 'What would I name my son?' he thought to himself.

Chapter 31

*R*yder spent the morning holding his son, bonding with him, and helping him grow. He struggled on what to name him and in the end, decided on a name that he hoped Seraphina would love. "Well Jackson Richard Durand, I have to go see Mommy, and make sure she's doing alright," he told his son very softly.

"You can take him to see her; that might help both of them" the nurse told him.

"That would be great; she's been struggling, and I know this little guy needs his mommy," he said to the nurse.

"I'm sure her milk will have come in and she will need him to start learning to nurse as well. His lungs are growing well, but he will need to stay on oxygen for a little longer," the nurse told him. "I'll prepare the mobile incubator for you, and you can take him with you."

'Maybe this will be better for her; once she sees Jackson, she might change her mind, and realize that he doesn't belong to Jason.' he thought to himself as he waited for the nurse to prepare the mobile incubator.

"Alright, once you get him to her room, you can take him out, and place him on Mom; remember, skin to skin is best, and if her milk has come in, try to get her to start nursing him; he might be a little slow picking up on it as preemies do sometimes have issues. Keep the oxygen going and he will be fine. Jackson needs to be back here in a little over an hour," the nurse told Ryder.

"Got it, thank you. Ok Jackson let's go see Mommy," he said softly, feeling elated, wheeling Jackson out of the NICU.

Ryder peeked in to see that Seraphina was awake and sitting up in bed looking out the window. He quietly walked in and wheeled their son into her room. She seemed lost in her thoughts as she had not heard Ryder, or the mobile incubator roll in.

He placed the incubator next to her bed, and lightly touched her arm bringing her back to the present. "Oh, you startled me," she said, turning to see Ryder.

"I'm sorry love, I thought you heard me," he said, feigning innocence. "Someone wants to meet you," he said as he moved out of the way, revealing their son. "This is our son Sera, Jackson Richard Durand, and he needs bonding time with his Mommy," he said as he opened the incubator, and gently took the baby out.

"Oh my god," she said, looking at the tiny bundle in blue. "He is beautiful."

"He is, open your gown love, he still needs skin to skin contact, and the nurse mentioned that if your milk has come in to try nursing him," he told her softly, bringing Jackson to her.

Seraphina was mesmerized by the baby and did what Ryder asked; opened the top of her gown, leaned back into the bed, and let Ryder place the baby against her chest, between her breasts.

"He looks exactly like you, coloring and everything; even his eyes are dark brown already," Ryder told her softly.

"I would have thought his coloring to be light, like Jason," she murmured.

Ryder sighed, "Seraphina, you and I have to talk for a bit, because it is killing me that you don't remember," he told her as they watched their son begin to root around, smelling his food, "I think he wants to nurse babe; place him at your breast, and tickle his lips with your nipple and I bet he will get the idea," Ryder told her.

Seraphina did that and within a few minutes, the baby latched on and began to nurse. Ryder watched in awe as the woman he loved, nursed their son, "This is the most amazing thing I have ever witnessed," he whispered as he moved in to kiss her. "I love you Sera, so much, and I want us to stay as the family we're meant to be."

"You said I don't remember; what is it that I don't remember?" she asked him, while watching the baby nurse.

"Please babe; think back to that night I signed the contract and how I took you back to your hotel and we were kissing," he told her softly, trying to help her remember that evening.

She nodded at the memory, thinking back to that night, his kisses were breaking down her barriers.

"Now think to the night we went out to dinner, and we returned to your room and had some drinks, and later, you took me to your bedroom to make love, and we did. It was the most amazing experience ever, and it's been killing me ever since I found out that Jason made a play for you as well," he told her softly, feeling his heart keenly.

"You are the only one I wanted, and the next time I saw you, it seemed like you didn't remember, or you had chosen not to say anything, so I didn't say anything because I feared that you would cancel the contract, because we made love. What I had not counted on was you getting pregnant," he said, hoping his words helped her to remember that amazing evening they had together.

"I don't remember; why can't I remember?" She asked him, trying to figure out why.

"Grant said, sometimes you take something to help you sleep and medications sometime muddle your brain. He thinks you having those drinks may have done the same thing to your brain, and why you don't remember," he replied.

"Hmm, let me think," she said as she continued to watch the baby nurse. She recounted again that first night, and them kissing. She managed to stop what they were doing and sent him home. She went to her room and got ready for bed, crawled in, and waited for sleep. She remembered that sleep had not come to her, as her body was still singing from Ryder's kisses, so she had gotten up, and took her sleep medication. While she waited for it to kick in, she could not stop thinking about Ryder, and how her body had responded to his kisses and touches. That brought her dreams of them alive and had been driving herself to distraction. She then brought up her memory of the night they went for dinner; the amazing food, and yes, the drinks they were having, and again her dreams were vivid, "I thought that was a dream," she said as her memory of them in her bed making passionate love, she thought was her dreaming. She was beginning to realize it was real; those dreams were memories.

"That night was no dream, you and I spent most of the night making love. I was smitten and already in love with you when you asked me. It never occurred to me that we had not used any kind of protection. I am sure Jackson is ours, and I have already asked for a paternity test to make sure. I told the doctor that while you were working, someone had taken advantage of you, and we wanted to be sure he was ours," Ryder told her.

Seraphina looked at Ryder and saw the seriousness in his face. "No wonder you've been pushing for the baby and mentioned it might not be a good idea for Kelley to take the baby," she said, beginning to put the pieces together, seeing the concern on his face.

"Kelley didn't know you and I had made love prior to Jason. Hell, I did not know that Jason had you until I found out you were pregnant. When I found out, I was shocked; and remembered that night, and realized we had not used anything. I was sure I was the father and asked Grant to confirm. When he told me it was likely Jason, I felt my heart fall through the floor, especially what he did to you. It started to dawn on me that you didn't remember and why you made all those plans to give the baby to Kelley," he told her, stroking her cheek seeing the war within her.

"It took everything I had to keep that night a secret; I didn't want to force it on you. I hoped you would have remembered on your own but had not. I was starting to panic when you told me you couldn't travel any more, that I would miss the birth, and lose the chance to find out if the baby was mine," he told her, wiping away the tears that started to spill from her cheeks.

"You would have been devastated if Kelley took the baby before you could have made things right," she said, finally finding her voice, warbled; unaware that their son had fallen asleep nursing.

"I would have and more; I'm sure I would have lost you forever," he told her, tears spilling down his cheeks. "I love you Seraphina, heart and soul, and I am so in love with Jackson. I want us to be a family, have more children, and grow old together. Please, tell me you want that too."

"Ryder, I love you more than I ever thought I could. I pushed so hard because I did not want to hurt more than I already was, and why I have tried to be so distant with anything related to the baby. Now, I am holding him, and I see him, and I know he's ours. Kelley is right like she always is, this baby is meant to be mine, as you are meant to be mine too," she said, feeling her heart begin to swell. "Yes, I want to grow old with you and have more babies, I want the whole package with you."

Ryder leaned in and kissed her hard. "Fantastic! When you've healed, I will properly propose, get married, and make more babies," he told her, before he kissed her again.

"Well, better not wait too long; I'm forty now, and my window for having babies is rapidly closing," she said, with a wink.

"Sweetheart, that will not be a problem at all," Ryder replied, with a huge grin. "You have another 20 minutes with Jackson before he has to go back to NICU. His lungs are just about there. The doc thinks a few more days and he might be good to come home."

"Awe, I don't want to let him go," she said softly, seeing him sleeping against her.

"I know love, you can visit him anytime you want; its encouraged, but don't push it because you're still healing too, alright? You have two areas that are trying to heal. The C-section incision, and the repair they did on your artery," he told her.

"Yea, I can feel them both quite keenly," she said, beginning to grimace in pain.

"Take it easy, Sera," Grant said, from the door. "I'm sure you can get some pain medication to help ease the pain."

"Yea, no kidding. Wow, this sucks," she muttered, with a grimace as she tried to move so she was a little more comfortable.

"Look at him; he sure is happy being on Mommy," Kelley said as she walked up to the bed. "I'm glad you're bonding with him; he needs his Mommy."

"So, I see. I'm sorry for being impossible, I honestly didn't know," Seraphina said to Kelley.

"I knew, as soon as I saw him, I knew he didn't belong to Jason, and wondered who else you were with. When I found out it was Ryder, it made sense to me, and why I am happy I do not have him. Besides, I have some news for you." Kelley said with a big grin.

"Oh, and that is?" Seraphina asked as she saw Grant get this huge grin on his face, "oh damn," she muttered with realization.

"Yup, we're pregnant!" Kelley said, excitedly. "And get this, its twins too!"

"Oh, holy shit; that's awesome news! I am so happy for you both." Seraphina said, laughing at Grant. "You do know that twins mean literally double everything; diapers, feeding, no sleep, crying, laundry and the whole gambit."

"It hasn't sunk in with him yet, just wait, and then he'll be crying the blues." Kelley said with a laugh, hugging Seraphina.

"This is awesome; I'm happy for you guys, and Sera and I will be getting married and making more babies too," Ryder piped up.

"What? You're engaged?" Grant said, wide-eyed.

"Not officially; I have to wait until she's healed and out of here. It will be a short engagement, and we will begin working on more babies as soon as we can." Ryder told them as he leaned in to kiss Seraphina.

"Even better," squealed Kelley, clapping with joy.

"You just want to plan my wedding," Seraphina said with a sigh. "She can't wait for Kayla, so she's just set her sights on us," she said to Ryder.

"It's fine love; there's only so much she can do growing twins, and you and I will do what we want," he told her. "I love you Sera, so much."

"I love you too Ryder," she replied with a long kiss.

Chapter 32

*E*ighteen months later:

"C'mon, this baby won't wait for your slow ass!" Reverberated throughout the entire house.

Ryder was in a slight panic as his wife was in labor. He had literally just gotten home from the track. One of his teams had won the race, and of course, that meant a lot of extra stuff, like the media question and answer session, the infamous hat dance, and photos.

"Sweet baby Jesus, Ryder! Let's go dammit, ow!" Seraphina yelled, before another contraction got the best of her. "Fuck, fuck, fuck..." she said as she did her breathing. When the contraction was over, she started walking towards the car. "Damn man, just might have to drive myself to the hospital. I have no idea what the hell he's doing," she muttered.

"I'm sorry my love, I really am, I'm here now, let's get you to the hospital," Ryder said, helping his wife into the car.

When he started the car, Seraphina gripped his one hand as she started her breathing, 'fuck, fuck, fuck..." she panted, under her breath.

"I don't think that's what we were taught in class," he said as he drove to the hospital as fast as he knew he could get away with.

"It helps me concentrate so stuff it, ow!" She replied, before starting her chant once again.

Ryder shook his head as he drove as fast as he could. "Wait, who has Jackson?" He asked, when he knew his wife could answer him.

"Kelley came by and took him on a play date with the twins; when I started labor, I told her to keep him as I had thought you were coming home sooner than you did. I thought you promised to keep your phone on and as soon I said labor, you'd come straight home, Ow fuck!" She said, gripping his free hand even tighter as she breathed. "Dammit, this baby is coming fast."

"We're two minutes out, we'll make it love. I am sorry, Jesse won and that meant I had duties to attend to, and I honestly forgot to check my phone in all the excitement. It wasn't until I was on the plane that I thought to even check my phone, and holy shit, I freaked when I saw your texts." Ryder told her, pulling into the hospital drop-off.

Ryder got out and waved over some help. "Hey, my wife's in labor and baby is coming fast," he said as he opened the passenger door.

A nurse and porter helped Seraphina into a wheelchair and took her in, "Meet her at labor and delivery," the nurse ordered Ryder before he could park the car, grab her bag and get up to his wife.

"I'm still a dead man," he muttered, knowing his wife was still mad at him. He had promised to help her get through labor and be the doting husband who helped his wife. He missed most of her laboring at home, and when he got home, it was already past time for her to go to the hospital.

Ryder ran up the stairs to labor and delivery and found his wife with ease. He helped her into a gown and then focused only on her, as she walked about the delivery suite. "God, this hurts," she said as she stopped, grabbing both of Ryder's hands, gripping them as she breathed.

"You're doing great love, you really are, and baby will be here in no time," he said, seeing the pain on his wife's face. It hurt him as he knew there was nothing he could do.

After several minutes, Dr. Bear walked in with a couple of nurses, "Hi Seraphina, how is labor coming along?" he asked, seeing his patient clench her teeth as she breathed.

"She's doing ok, but she's in a lot of pain," Ryder told their doc.

"Ok, Seraphina, let's check you and see how much longer this is going to be," Dr. Bear said, both he and Ryder helped Seraphina to the bed. "Ok, Seraphina, you're at ten which is awesome, so, while we get everything ready, you listen to your body, and when you feel that immense pressure we talked about, take a huge breath, and push as hard as you can," Dr. Bear told her as a lot of activity suddenly happened around the couple.

"You've got this love; I love you, and you can do this," Ryder said softly, before kissing her and stroking her hair.

Seraphina had a firm grip on Ryder's hand and did not let go while she listened to her body and pushed as hard as she could. Ryder felt immense pain, his wife crushed his hand as she pushed, but there was no way he was going to tell her that; she was literally pushing a human being out of her body.

"That was a fantastic push, Seraphina; a few more like that and the head will be out," Dr. Bear guided, waiting for her body to contract again, pushing the baby out from her body.

Seraphina pushed with everything she had, and once the baby was born, she fell back, feeling incredibly exhausted. "You my love, are my hero. You did it, she's here, and she's perfect." Ryder told her, before kissing her hard.

"Fantastic job Seraphina, I want you to rest and let us take over; Ryder, go and stay with baby, I have to stay here with Seraphina to make sure her body does what it's supposed to," Dr. Bear said, keeping a close watch on his patient. He knew that this birth would require special attention. One, his patient was on the older side creating potential issues, and second, this was her first natural birth after C-section, which can also create some issues with the body not doing what it's supposed to.

A couple of hours later, Seraphina was settled into a room, with her newborn daughter in her arms. She was exhausted on a level she had never known existed, and yet she was very happy. She was quietly bonding with her daughter, when she heard the door open and saw Ryder peek in. "There you are, I was wondering what happened to you," she said, with a smirk.

Ryder walked into the room with a very large bouquet of flowers, and a small box in his other hand. "I'm sorry my love; back at the house, I was trying to remember where I had hidden your gift, and in the panic I forgot. That's what was taking me so long, and I knew you were getting more anxious and so mad at me. So, I had to duck out, and go back to the house to find this," he said, holding up the box. "I had this made for you when you told me we were having another baby. You have made me the happiest man ever! I love you, cherish you, adore you, and I have the hots for you," he said as he gave her the box, and she gave him their daughter.

"Oh sweetheart, you didn't have to," she started.

"No. I did have to; you've been through hell, and it took a lot for you to let me into a place no one else was allowed. I am thankful that even after everything, you chose me. You could have told me no, could have decided upon another yahoo, or you could have sworn off men forever. You said yes to a relationship with me, and now we have two children, an amazing marriage, and I hope that I make you as happy as you've made me," he told her as he watched her open the gift.

Inside the box, was a very special necklace; it was like a family tree, but her birthstone was in the center and next to that was Ryder's birthstone, at the roots of the tree. On the branches were two stones, one for Jackson's birth and the second was for Sierra Grace, their newborn daughter. There were a few more branches that were empty but could be adorned with stones.

Seraphina looked at the necklace, and knew the meaning behind it, and then looked up at her husband, who was watching her, "This is incredible, thank you," she said. "But I have a question for you, just how many children do you want? I see more branches and I don't think I'll be having that many babies," she said, thinking.

"Well, sweetheart, we don't know how many more we will have, but with the way you and I make love, you have to admit, anything is possible," he said, with a grin, before leaning in to kiss his beautiful wife.

The End.